A Game of Vows and Vendettas

GIRL GAMES
BOOK FOUR

RUBY ROE

ALSO BY RUBY ROE

Girl Games Series

A Game of Hearts and Heists

A Game of Romance and Ruin

A Game of Deceit and Desire

A Game of Love and Hate

A Game of Parties and Proposals

A Game of Vows and Vendettas

A Game of Brats and Brides

Kingdom of Immortal Lovers Series

House of Crimson Hearts

House of Crimson Kisses

House of Crimson Curses

House of Crimson Nights

House of Crimson Spice

Deals of Dark Desire

Architecti

Interitus

To every reader who ~~begged, pleaded, coaxed~~ *bullied me into writing* **The Wedding***, this is your fault. I hope you're happy.*

This book is my love letter to you, the reader. It is my thanks, my gratitude, and my eternal dedication to the community. I packed it full of Easter eggs and all the tropey fun you'd expect from a crossover story.

With thanks to all the Kickstarter backers for helping to bring this book to life. And in particular, for the incredible level of support from Alexis, Katrina, Fayte, and Atar Sara.

CHAPTER 1

PENELOPE

THREE WEEKS AGO

On reflection, illegally escaping out of New Imperium and into Sangui City—a city, I might add, that is full of vampires that have hated magicians for the last thousand years—was probably not my best idea. Especially when you consider that I'm a magician princess.

But I'm here now, and I stole some vampire pheromone thingy that Bella—one of my sister's friends—had lying around. So, I'm pretty sure I'll just look like any other human and smell like a vampire recently took a chunk out of me.

Undetectable, right?

Or, that is the plan. I tried to wear an outfit that made me look like a hunter, some disgusting combat trousers and a jacket. My lovely long blonde hair pinned up to within an inch of its life. I look wretched, no pink, no dress in sight. But at least I'm incognito.

I walk through the Whisper Club. It's owned by Octavia

Beaumont, one of the original vampires and through some tenuous link between Bella, my sister, and their friends, they all know each other. Which is why the vampires are coming to the wedding. A historic occasion and the first of probably many, given Mother wants to work on peace negotiations and to open up trade formally between our cities.

The club is huge. Corridors and offset rooms scatter the walls. I walk down a set of stairs from a mezzanine area into the main club room that's set into a circular hollow. The lights are so dim they obscure the dancers until they're nothing but a mass of writhing shadows.

The odd flash of fang glints in the roving spotlights. It furls my stomach into the tightest knots. There's something about vampires. They disgust and allure me in equal measure. I pass a couple, one human and one vampire. He fucks her against the wall, pumping in and out of her while her leg wraps around his waist. But it's when he sinks his fangs into her throat that her head rolls back, and a guttural moan of pleasure escapes.

It does things to me, watching the drip of blood roll between his lips and the way she digs her nails into his back. They're connected, moving as one. A part of me covets it, wonders what it would be like to do something so sordid. The rest of me is sickened. This suddenly feels like the stupidest idea I ever had. What if I'm caught? What if someone realises who I am and uses it to blackmail my family?

But what choice did I have?

I should explain. Roman Oleg was set to marry my sister—one of these 'decided at birth' things'. But turns out Morrigan is a raging lesbian and had zero intention of ever marrying him. Also, he's a giant cunt. So, there's that. Now, my sister and I haven't ever gotten on. She's just so... ugh. Studious, nerdy, planned to perfection every. Single. Time. Drives me bonkers. We argue, like a lot, and I... maybe... sort of spite dated him.

Look, I'm not proud, it happened. And much to my chagrin, she was right, he was a total shithead.

And when I say shithead, I mean the kind of I'm-going-to-plot-to-over-throw-the-entire-monarchy type shithead. Thankfully, my sister and her gang of friends managed to capture him. He was tried and promptly shipped off to the vampires to live out his life as a blood bag.

Hence, the Whisper Club.

But during that brief period I dated him, I snooped in his files—yes, alright, another example of poor decision making on my part.

But I found a trio of magician lords who all wanted something from the other. Bear with me while I explain:

Lord Jeremiah wanted a patch of fertile Sangui Cupa-growing land that was owned by one Lord Mosel. Mosel was after some trading contracts with the fae that were owned by Lord Brinkley. And this is where I excited myself because Brinkley was after dying mansion magic that the one and only Lord Jeremiah possessed.

I mean, come on, it was perfect:

Jeremiah would give Brinkley the magic and would receive the land from Mosel. Mosel would get the trading contract from Brinkley and give Jeremiah the land. And Brinkley would get the mansion magic from Jeremiah in exchange for handing over the fae contacts.

It's a head fuck, but it worked. And I thought that maybe, just maybe, if I could arrange this, then I'd garner a bit of respect from the palace and Mother's council... and my sister. Maybe I'd be taken seriously for once. I'd be worth more than just being the spare heir.

It was a good plan. Until it went to shit.

Neither Brinkley, Mosel nor Jeremiah would give their portion of the deal without first receiving what they were after. I hit a giant stalemate, and it's not like I can tell the queen, or even ask Stirling—my sister's fiancé and master negotiator—for help, they'd all be 'blah blah blahing' me over having attempted to do this in the first place. I can see it now, them lecturing and boring me to death over why I shouldn't meddle with palace affairs.

Don't they realise how dull my life is? What is the spare even meant to do? Nothing. Just exist. We're never needed, and we're always in the way.

Probably why, as I stride past another vampire, the temptation to insert myself into the most taboo position I can floods my system.

No, Penelope, these creatures are killers. And yet, every human I walk past seems to be having the orgasm of a lifetime. Have we been wrong about them for the last millennium?

Either way, I'm here now, having snuck into probably the most dangerous place in the realm for a magician princess, and worse, about to get on my knees for my criminal ex-boyfriend to beg for a solution.

Fuck. This really is a low point.

The club smells like most clubs in New Imperium: eau du sweaty body, booze-soaked floors and the hint of sex. It's the faint stench of something metallic that unnerves me.

I make my way into the heart of the club. Bodies tussle and shove me as I weave my way around the dance floor, past the bar and into a second dance area. With my back pressed into the wall so no one can come at me, I scan every inch of the room, searching for where they keep the blood bags. But there's not enough light to differentiate human from hunter from vampire. I keep moving, trying to steady my heart, which feels like it's going to thump out of my chest.

I need to do better, having my blood pump this fast is only going to attract unwanted attention.

I slip around another vampire and whoever its feeding on and finally spot Roman.

He looks horrendous, no wonder I couldn't find him. He's hardly recognisable, save for his enormous stature and mop of wavy dark hair. Though it's more limp and lacklustre than waves or locks. But it's his eyes that are the most startling. He used to have these dark infinite pools, so cold and endless. They'd suck you in, as inevitable as death. But now they're small and beady and the kind of shallow that barely holds a shadow of his former power.

He's handcuffed to a chair, blood smothers his shirt, several puncture marks litter his arms and neck, he carries purple bags under his eyes and cracks on his lips like he was born with them.

I almost feel sorry for him... almost.

But he tried to take everything from Morrigan, steal the crown and screw my family, and all while using me in the process, so he can go royally fuck himself.

I hang back until the vampire feeding from him unlatches and saunters into the club.

When no one else approaches him, I take my chance. He's handcuffed so I'm safe enough. His head hangs limp.

"Roman," I spit, pouring as much venom into my words as I can.

His head snaps up, his gaze unfocused as he tries to put

two and two together. Of course I'd be the last person he expected to see.

"Pen?" he breathes, his words scratchy and hoarse.

"Yeah, Roman, it's me."

He tries to sit up straighter; his neck oozes blood, and I can't help the way my lip curls and my nose wrinkles. I might have a sordid fascination with the plague that is vampires, but his neck is frankly gross.

"Some things are worse than death, trust me," he says and tries to laugh, but his neck oozes with each choked huff.

I swallow down a gag. "Gods, just stop talking for a second and listen. I need your help."

His dark little eyes widen and then narrow. There's a flash and I know it's the moment he starts scheming.

"Don't even try and manipulate me, Roman, you're not in a position to ask for anything," I snarl.

"And yet, it seems you are in need of help, little princess. Tell me, what is it I can do for you?"

I scan his features looking for the lie, the scheme, but I can't read anything other than curiosity.

I take a breath and explain. "I brokered a deal between three of your contacts, Lord Jeremiah, Mosel and Brinkley."

"You...? Sorry, what?" he says, his eyebrows bunching.

"Oh, give over, is it really that surprising? I'm not entirely useless," I snap.

Wait, I'm not, am I?

Gods, is that really what everyone thinks of me? Even Roman, at his fucking lowest, with no hope of escape, no contacts and facing certain death, thinks he's more resourceful than me?

"I mean..." he starts, and then shakes his head,

changing his mind about whatever he was going to say. "If you brokered a deal, why do you need my help?"

My shoulders sag. "I'm at a stalemate. None of them will hand over their property or contracts without getting what they asked for. And I don't have any dirt on any of them to force their hand. I figured you always had dirt on your clients."

He sits even straighter in his chair, pushing his shoulders back, that nasty little glint in his eye glimmering back to life.

"And what makes you think I'll share anything useful? What's in it for me?"

Is he for real? No pretence, straight for the payoff. I suppose I shouldn't be surprised. "I'm not helping you escape, if that's what you think. I'm not stupid."

He sneers at me. I expected this. As if Roman would ever do anything out of the kindness of his heart. I lean close to him. "Rumour has it, Marcel was taken to a different club. What if I promise to get your brother a message?"

Marcel was working with Roman to overthrow our family and steal the crown. He was sentenced the same as Roman. But he was recently moved to another club.

Roman looks me up and down with so much disdain, it peels away every layer of confidence I had.

I grit my teeth and stand firm. "Don't fucking look at me like that, do you want in or not?"

He presses his lips together and then gestures for me to lean close. I don't trust him one bit. Not one fucking bit.

But this is what I came for. So, what choice do I have? I hate that that is becoming a mantra.

I do as he asks and move to hover just above his neck. Anyone glancing our way would think I was feeding. His skin smells salty and stale, that deep unwashed dirt that only skin can hold. But it's the energy he gives off that makes my skin bristle. Round goosebumps rise up my flesh. Morrigan was right, this man is evil to his core. It literally billows off him.

I stay there, my heart pounding as he makes me wait and wait. And wait.

Right as I'm about to step back he says, "You know the thing about you, Pen? For all your beauty and allure..."

"Get to the point."

He laughs, a nasty sneer of a thing that crawls down my spine like the clack, clack, clack of scorpion pincers.

He jerks suddenly. There's a clank and a crunch as metal buckles. I yelp; he catches me. He must have ripped his arms from the cuffs. He grips the back of my head and pulls me in for a kiss.

His breath is worse than his skin, full of decaying, unwashed teeth. I scream and gag as he presses his filthy mouth against mine.

I claw at his face, slapping and scratching at him. But he holds me tight.

I bite down on his lip. He growls, shoves me back so hard I crash to the floor. A gang of vampires piles on top of him. Pinning him. But he fights back, smashing faces and breaking jaws. Blood, bone and tissue splatter the floor and furniture. Finally, they drain him until he passes out or hopefully fucking dies. They drag his blood-covered body away. None of the vampires look too healthy, but I guess they'll heal a lot faster than him. If he even does. He looks grey. Gods, I hope he's fucking dead.

I brush myself down, my outfit is squiffy, my hair a mangled mess of tufts and pins half fallen out.

A shadow looms above me. I peer up; it's a woman

holding her hand out. I take it and she hauls me up, only for me to realise too late how cool her skin is.

Cool enough to be a vampire.

She cocks her head at me, chin-length hair cut into a suave set of waves. Her features are chiselled, her body muscled. What stops me breathing though, are her eyes. So potent, so dark and the strangest mix of chaos and curiosity. She's stunning. I've only been with one woman, but gods, if she were a magician, I'd genuinely consider getting on my knees for her. The way she stares at me sets a fire blazing in my stomach.

"What are you?" she says.

"Pardon?"

"You smell like a vampire but look like a human. So, stranger, I'll ask you again... what are you and how do you know Roman?"

She takes a step closer; I step back. She moves forward, again and again until my back hits the wall. Then, she places her palms either side of my head, pinning me in place.

Fuck. The fire in my gut turns to adrenaline, butterflies dancing, and I'm not sure why. Fear or fury or a furnace of desire?

My heart pounds so loud it throbs in my ears. Fuck. Fuck. This is exactly why I shouldn't have come here. I know what she is. What she could do to me.

Gods... what *could* she do to me? A vision of the vampire and human fucking as I entered flashes through my head. I need to get a fucking grip. She could just as easily snap my neck.

"I... I shouldn't be here," I stutter out, my fingers and toes tingling with the urge to run. I don't know who she is, but I do know she's a predator.

"Is that so? Secrets to hide, hmm?" Her voice is silky. My heart rate slows, steadies until I feel like I have control again. Did she do that? Is she doing that thing? Fuck. What was it Quinn said. Compulsion?

"What if I do? I heard this club keeps everyone's secrets..." I say, my confidence returning. I'm a fucking princess, after all; I'm not going to be dictated to by some vampire trash.

"Quite the attitude for a stranger who shouldn't be here and currently has no way of escaping..."

"There's always a way," I say and draw my knee up and ram it into her stomach.

She lurches forward, her palms slipping off the wall enough for me to dash out of her grip.

I make it five feet.

Five.

Before she yanks me by the wrist and spins me, pinning my back to her chest. She sinks into the shadows, taking me with her.

Shit.

"I'm going to ask you again, who the fuck are you?" she breathes into my ear.

Adrenaline spikes through me. I should be running, screaming. But I'm frozen in place, desperate to know if I'll end up like that human girl: fucked, bitten, orgasming for days. It's so wrong. So. Fucking. Wrong. And yet my pussy clamps down, my underwear sticking to me.

The vampire leans in, inhaling.

What the hell? She's literally sniffing me. Oh gods, I hope she can't smell my arousal.

The only option is hardball. "Do you get off on this? Pinning women in place and forcing them to do whatever you want?"

"What if I do? This club is designed to dish out your darkest desires, *Stranger*. So tell me... have you ever fucked a vampire?"

She smelt my arousal, then. Shit. My heart rate quickens. She must be able to sense the thudding beat because I hear the smile in her sneer. "I'll take that as a no, but you want to."

I lunge forward and shove back, smashing her into the wall hard enough she releases me. Spinning around, I face her, knowing that if I try and run, she will just catch me again. I have to think my way out of this. She's masc. I can tell from the air of confidence filling her gaze and jutting her jaw. The muscles bulging under her shirt are a giveaway too. The question is, is she also a dom?

"I see you're the kind of brat that likes to fight back..." she says.

Yes. Then. And I'd bet money on the fact she likes to tame a brat. This is my play. "What's your name?" I ask.

"Dahlia. What about you, Princess?"

I smile. She has no idea. "I think I'm rather fond of Princess."

She cocks her eyebrow at me. "Hilarious. The cute blonde brat fancies herself a real-life princess, hey?"

"Something like that." I shrug.

She folds her arms and looks me up and down. "I could just torture your secrets out of you. Spank you until you tell me exactly what you're doing... Or maybe I'm in the mood for real torture, it is one of my kinks..."

She watches me swallow that information. I force myself not to tremble, to breathe slow and deep. She likes a brat. And I am the brattiest of them all. I just need to be me.

I take too long to respond. She grabs me by the arms and pins me against the wall. We're face to face. Oh gods.

The last vestiges of very sensible and needed fear vanish. She's hot, she's masc and from the way she's pinning me against the wall, she's clearly a dom. I should absolutely not be fantasising about her fucking me like this.

What I need to do is locate a heavy dose of panic. Maybe throw out a few first-class screams. Running for my life is probably sensible.

And yet I do absolutely none of those.

What in the ever-loving fuck is wrong with me? But the more I think about how much danger I'm in, the wetter I'm getting.

"You're lucky I'm feeling generous, and I can tell you're just a human. Albeit a very nice smelling one."

She leans so close our breath mingles, my skin heats, goosebumps rise, but this time not from disgust, but lust. I should be ashamed of myself. Their species killed thousands of ours. My eyes fall to her lips. All I want is to place mine on hers.

Fuck.

She grabs each of my wrists in turn and grips them above my head. Then she pushes her knee between my legs and drives her thigh up to meet my cunt.

"Oh. Oh fuck," I say as heat pools between my legs. "I... we..."

Can she feel how wet I am through my underwear and pants? Her eyes glimmer, hooded desire making them heavy and my stomach flutter. I need to get out of here. This was a bad idea. I failed to get what I came for, and Roman is no longer an option. I need to cut my losses and run before anyone discovers who I really am.

"Dahlia... let me go, please...?"

The words snap her out of her daze. She stares at me, her eyes drooping, something passing through them.

What was it? Regret? Sadness? It's gone before I can place it.

I'm sensing a pattern with myself—one filled with things that seem like a good idea. But I'm never coming back here. Aside from Octavia at the wedding, I doubt I'll ever meet another vampire. I'm probably about to die, they'll just make another spare heir anyway.

Oh, what the hell...

I slide my hand to her jaw and pull her in.

Our lips meet, a frisson of electricity passing between us, like fireworks and lightning. Like a summer breeze and fresh snowfall. She smells like bergamot and rich spices and winter winds. Her hands paw at my waist, my back, she holds me like I'm treasure and diamonds. Gods, I've never been kissed like this. She deepens the embrace, her strong hands pulling me closer, harder. Holding me.

No.

It's more than that. It's like she owns me, as if I've only ever been hers.

Fuck.

If this is what kissing a vampire is like, no fucking wonder that woman looked like she'd died and gone to heaven. My body melts against Dahlia. I sink into her, giving myself over to her, silently pleading with her to take more of me, own more of me.

My fingers find their way into her raven waves and tug. She groans against me, so I pull harder. I want more. I need to drown in this. Her mouth opens, and I slide my tongue against hers. Everywhere we touch ignites with heat and electricity. Molten want courses like energy between us. Her fingers glide over my breasts, my nipples harden in response.

I don't want this to stop. But it has to. This was

supposed to be my distraction. I kissed her to make her let me go.

I need to get out.

Roman screwed me.

I don't know what I expected but I should have known better.

This was all a mistake.

I pull away. Suck her bottom lip between my teeth and let it pop back as I release her.

"Fuck." She says it like a growl rumbling between her ribs.

"Yeah. That was..." I say but struggle to find the right words.

"It really was," she says.

I give her one final glance. "I have to go."

"Don't," she says, and for the barest of moments, I swear I see a flash of softness in her gaze.

"I can't stay," I say, my stomach knotting, this time, with regret. I wish I could, but what use would it be telling her?

"Will you come back?"

I shake my head.

Whatever softness I saw vanishes as I slip into the darkness of the club and away, back to New Imperium with one word, one taste, one feeling burnt into my memory: Dahlia.

CHAPTER 2

DAHLIA

I hate weddings. In fact, I hate romance too. Women aren't worth it. Far too high maintenance.

Fucking? The occasional orgasm? Now that's worth it. But I'm yet to find a woman that doesn't bore me to tears after five minutes in her company. So for now, I will grin and bear this farce of a wedding we're heading to for 'diplomatic reasons'. And hope I can find some delicious magician pussy to taste.

I peer out of the carriage window.

"Do lighten up, Dahlia, you look like you sucked a lemon," Xavier says. I give him the middle finger and kick my legs up onto the seat opposite.

Octavia promptly shoves my feet off. "Manners, we're about to be in the presence of royalty."

Red nods like she gives a shit. I eyeball her in response and her mouth quirks. Dick.

This place is her second home, she doesn't care about airs and graces. It's not like she's even dressed up. Red's wearing Hunter Academy combats, her shaggy blonde hair is a mess as usual and her undercut needs trimming! At least Octavia made an effort, she's wearing a slimline black suit with a corseted waistcoat. Her long hair has been styled into luscious waves, and she's even wearing a rouge lipstick that matches the colour of her eyes.

I glare at Red and then shoot a poisonous one at Octavia. "I'm allergic to weddings."

Gabriel, my twin brother, dressed in his usual blood-red suit, is curled up in the opposite corner of the carriage, a book in his hand and three by his feet. He doesn't bother to look up at me when he says, "No, you just haven't found a woman high maintenance enough to keep you on your toes."

I waft a shocked palm over my mouth. "I don't like high-maintenance women."

"Yes, you do," comes a chorus from all four of them.

I open my mouth and close it again. They're probably right. "Oh, fuck off, the lot of you."

Xavier pulls a hand through his raven locks. We're not blood related—well, Gabriel and I are—but the rest of us aren't. We're vampire family and yet we all carry the same dark hair, chiselled jaws and ego for days. I've always resented the fact our hairstyles are so similar. Regardless of our stunning hair, Xavier seems to have a death wish today. He leans forward and plucks one of Gabriel's books off the floor and opens the cover. Gabriel—in a feat of speed I don't think I've ever seen—lunges forward and wrenches the book out of Xavier's hands, then taps him across the cheek with it. It's a gentle slap, but hard enough to make Xavier's locks bounce around his head and scruff his long coat collar.

Ooft.

Red and I share a glance. It almost kills me. She looks away, and I fold my lips inside my mouth trying to eat the laugh threatening to spill out. Xavier, utterly fucking dumbstruck, let's his jaw hang loose.

Gabriel shimmies in his seat, straightening up. "Who does that? Who just takes someone's book without asking? Get a grip of yourself, Xavier."

Finally, Xavier blinks the shock away. "You might be my brother, but I will beat you to a pulp if you lay another finger on me."

Gabriel's mouth twitches, but he doesn't deign to look at Xavier. Instead, he keeps his eyes firmly on the words in front of him, which only serves to piss Xavier off further. He glowers at Gabriel, his upper lip curling, a fang dropping.

Octavia touches his forearm, and he snaps out of it.

I rest an arm on Gabriel's leg, unsure whether it's comfort for me or protection from Xavier. Gabriel has been more aloof than normal of late. Since he and Keir broke up, he's drowned himself in his books and research. I rub his leg. I'm not affectionate with my other siblings, but Gabriel and I shared a womb. He's the only one of my blood relatives alive and just being with him is a sort of solace.

My mind wanders to Sadie, a constant void in our family dynamic. With Mother now human, that void won't be filled with another child. Mother was one of the original three vampires, along with Octavia and Isabella. But it all got a bit messy a few months ago. Millennia-old secrets and vendettas were revealed and, well, Sadie got caught up in it.

Gabriel swats me away and draws his legs up under his chin. My eyes dart to the empty space. The space for Sadie. It's the same at home, always a spare seat. None of us have actually talked about it, but we seem to have agreed that keeping a chair at our tables is the right thing to do. It's like none of us can quite accept she's gone.

Of course, Octavia does our family dinners now, not

Mother. She's too busy boning her new missus in Ora City. They're teaching and studying at some morbid university. Fin? No. Finis Academy, I think it's called.

Anyway, I haven't visited yet. She's asked, but what with building the new training facilities in the Hunter Academy, the odd guarding job I've had to do plus integrating the hunter and vampire armies into one, I've not had a free second.

As if reading my thoughts, Octavia's crimson-coloured eyes drift to the empty seat. Her features stiffen.

I open my mouth to ask if she's alright, but Red slides her hand into Octavia's and asks her something mundane.

I sling my ankle over my knee and fold my arms, staring into the darkness of the tunnels. I'm already over this trip. I'll be missing three workouts and two nights out with the lads, and for what? Some dumb princess wedding and the façade of political niceties? I get that this is Octavia's thing, but why did she have to drag us into it?

"Right," Octavia says, producing a stack of paper. "These are the royals. I want you to memorise their names and faces." She hands everyone a set of documents, and my eyes scan the images.

They all look delightfully bland until...

There's a slender blonde in one of the images. A blonde I recognise.

You have got to be kidding me...

CHAPTER 3

PENELOPE

Rule number one of being the spare: never expect people to like you.

Of course they don't. You're just the other one: a 'break glass in case of emergency' kinda gal.

And that's aside from the fact I'm a constant irritation to Morrigan, and she's everyone's favourite.

Obviously. I mean she *is* the heir apparent.

I draw pink over my lips and huff as I glance in my ensuite mirror. It's not the right shade. I hunt through my makeup bag and pull another one out. Powder puff, it should match my designer baby pink heels and dress. But when I draw it over my lips it still isn't right.

I huff in the mirror and clap my balled fists together, drawing my index finger over my knuckles, and then tap my little finger on the pads of my other middle and index fingers. The thinnest most pathetic thread of magic peels from the palace wall.

"Oh, come on, I actually tried," I whine, knowing damn well the palace isn't going to answer. The silvery thread drifts through the air and lands on my mouth. My lips shimmer and tingle, and when they settle, my lipstick is finally the correct colour. I stroke the wall in thanks.

I examine myself, pout, and smile, pleased that my lips match the dress. The designer sent it to me, asked if I'd wear it out and be photographed. I was only too happy to oblige, of course, given the way the dress clings to my figure.

It's a dream. Fits like a glove. Cut short, curving around my ass, and displaying my ugly long legs. That's another thing Morrigan got. Curves. And the same figure and olive skin to die for as our mother, while I got gangly limbs, our father's pasty white skin and equally boring blonde hair. Even the blue of my eyes is basic. It's not like I can do anything about it either. I'm no good at hair-dying magic, unlike my sister. I can manage the odd lip tint and occasionally manage to reheat food when I've taken too long to eat. I've got maybe a dozen pieces of magic under my belt and not a single fucking Collection tattoo.

Unlike Morrigan, who has gone and studied in all the top mansions, castles and palaces in the realm. In record time she's learned enough that the mansions have bestowed upon her a Collection tattoo, meaning she has unrestricted access to their magic.

And I've got nothing.

Which is precisely why I'll eat a barrel of Borderlands dirt before I ask her for help changing my hair colour. And that is why my hair stays platinum blonde and hers is as dark as the night sky.

I sigh as I stare into the mirror, dissatisfied as usual. My watch tells me it's time to go. I exit the bathroom and head to my bedroom desk. My fingers brush the letters strewn over it.

I'd like to tell you they're some sort of romantic love

letters. Invitations to swanky parties or, gods only know what. But they're so much worse. I shuffle some papers over the top to hide them.

To hide my secret.

My fuck-up.

It should have worked. It could have if the lords had all played ball. If Roman would have just given me something... anything. I swear I'd have delivered a message to his brother too. But no. Well, fuck him. He's probably dead now anyway.

I'm just gutted because this would have been my first real achievement in palace politics. But no. The only person who ever gets credit for anything is Morrigan.

I shuffle the papers again, realising I probably should have told someone. But what good would it do? It's not like they're going to follow up on the threats. It's just all pomp and ego. Trying to force me to fix their mess.

A knock on the door startles me as I brush the last of the letters away.

Benedict, Mother's chief of staff, is by the door. "Your Highness, the carriage awaits for the family meal this evening."

Joy.

"I'm not going."

Benedict gives a nervous laugh. He brushes a hand over his moustache. "While I'd love to entertain your antics this evening, Ms Penelope, I'm afraid the consequences would be too severe for the pair of us. Her Royal Highness Queen Calandra was adamant that you should attend."

I grit my teeth.

His eyes drop to his jacket pocket and he pulls out a letter. "I'm afraid I need to inform you that I found this."

Shit.

No one knows about the letters. They've been finding their way into the palace or into my carriages without going through the royal postal system for a couple of weeks. I thought I was keeping them secret.

Benedict's eyes skirt from me to the letter, his brow rising. "So this wasn't the first one. You already know?" His tone is low, not a threat exactly. And not a warning either. More like a mildly irritated protectiveness.

"I..." I start.

Oh, fuck me. This isn't good. The truth is, I never wanted to date Roman. I did it to piss Morrigan off.

Obviously.

And I saw an opportunity and thought I could use his contacts to my benefit. I figured it had been long enough since he was banished that it would look like it was my doing. It's not like I expected the lords to get pissed enough to send me death threats.

I just wanted to do something better than Morrigan for once. She gets everything. She's the heir; I'm just the spare in case something happens to her. I'm not important.

Not wanted.

Not needed.

Do you have any idea how much that shit can fuck a girl's psyche up? It's not like I stand a chance against her. Look at her... Total overachiever. Power seeping from every pore in her body. Born a queen.

I am, in essence, useless.

So, call a bitch crazy, but I took whatever opportunity I could find. But apparently, I've fucked up...

And sure, I probably shouldn't have gone to visit Roman in Sangui City. Gods forbid anyone actually found out. But I was cornered and needed help. The plus side of seeing him get his comeuppance wasn't too bad either.

Besides, it's not like anyone noticed I'd left New Imperium, and it was only one night.

Benedict coughs, drawing my attention back to him. His eyes fall away from mine as he holds the letter out.

"It's not the original," I say.

He nods, solemn. "It's a copy."

I knew it. The writing isn't in red. It's in muted black, like a magician used replicating magic on it. But if that's not the original...

"Benedict...Where is the original?" I *do* threaten him with my tone.

"I'm sorry, Your Highness, but I had no choice," his voice is now a whine.

I knead my temples. "Tell me you didn't go to Daria?"

"This is your life we're talking about," Benedict says.

I snatch the letter out of his hands. I hope it gives him a paper cut and really hurts. "Is it? Or are you just worried about Morrigan's wedding?"

His eyes widen like carriage wheels, he pouts and then touches my arm, completely ignoring my comment. "You must attend this evening."

I grumble but he vanishes down the corridor knowing I'll acquiesce.

I nearly leap out of my skin as I turn back to the door only to come face to face with Daria herself, who halts close enough I actually have to crane my neck to look up at her, and I'm tall.

"Daria," I say, twitching and knowing full well I'm about to be scalded.

Daria is severe. Her features are sharp and angular. Like her sense of humour. Bracing, cutting, and only funny when you're not on the receiving end of it. She is the only topic Morrigan and I actually agree on. The woman is as vicious as she is feral, but it's what makes her good at her job.

"Your Highness," she says, staring down the blade point of her nose at me.

"What can I do for you on this lovely evening?" Of course, I know exactly what I can do for her, and this evening is turning out to be anything but lovely. But I'm not giving her an opening if I don't have to.

"Must we play games? This is quite the serious matter."

Oh please, I only ever play games, and she damn well knows it. But her face remains utterly devoid of emotion. So boring.

Fine. "Have you told Calandra?" I ask.

This time, Daria twitches. Interesting, so Mother doesn't know.

"Do I need to tell her? How serious is this?" she asks.

Serious enough that I probably need to give royal land away, embezzle money and beg Stirling to make the deal of a lifetime, but no big, honestly.

"It's fine. It's probably just some fan boy wishing he could get a piece of me."

Daria's eyes narrow to slits.

I tuck the letter into my handbag. "I'm going to be late. Is there anything else?"

"How long has it been going on?"

"Not long." Half a lie. It's been going on two straight weeks.

"I'm launching an investigation. And you're getting a bodyguard. A personal one."

"I don't need a fucking babysitter. It's just some city boy desperate for attention."

Daria leans down into my face. "Your safety is my

concern. Not which fanboy wants to slip his todger in your knickers."

I open my mouth but all that comes out is a stifled cough-laugh. The word todger should not be allowed in the mouth of someone so stern.

She continues, ignoring my lip twitch. "There will be no protesting. You will take the bodyguard, or I will personally chain you to this room. And given the imminency of the royal wedding, I think we both know which Calandra would prefer. Understood?"

I press my lips together to stop the scream from coming out and nod. But not before giving her a sly birdie as I march down to the palace vestibule. Was it childish? Probably. Did it make me feel better? Absolutely.

My new bodyguard is standing by the carriage. His arm out wide, indicating I should get in. He looks like he's eighty. Wrinkled, hunched over and as beige as the clothes he's wearing.

Fucking great.

CHAPTER 4
PENELOPE

As predicted, this welcome party is dull as fuck. Morrigan, though, seems pleased with the proceedings, and our 'honoured' guests are arriving any second now.

"When they arrive, you will be polite," my mother says.

We're in some restaurant cum bar at the edge of the city with expensive, lavish chandeliers hanging from the ceiling. They glitter and charm the eye. A drink will cost you an obscene amount of coin. So the only people in here are the wealthy and the filthy rich. Mother ensured the welcome party included the elite, the noble and the magically powerful. In other words, friends of the palace.

She didn't want to risk an outburst or fight breaking out either, so everyone has been prepped, checked, and primed to within an inch of their lives.

Servers are dressed in a black-and-white uniform that looks like it was starched to death. The atmosphere in here is the perfect blend of sensual rouge lighting: not too bright as to bleach the air, but not so dim you struggle to see the face you're talking to. The tables are full of hor d'oeuvres and there are even bottles of blood imported from Sangui. That was a particularly well thought out idea on Mother's part. I'll give her dues, she's prepped well. I just wish the bar wasn't full of people. But that is a decidedly me problem. I can't seem to help myself. I piss off almost everyone I meet.

Morrigan was right about one thing; I'm more preoccupied with clothes than humans—at least they're nice to me.

"They're due any minute now," Mother says, her eyes feverishly glancing to the door. She grabs a glass of champagne off a passing server's tray and guzzles half of it.

She thought it was sensible to meet the vampires on neutral ground. Though what is neutral about a bar full of drunk magician idiots who have consumed more Sangui Cupa than they have blood in their body is beyond me. We're in New Imperium for goodness' sake. Neutral territory would have been the tunnels. Not that I can tell anyone I've been in them or know anything about them.

I catch a glimpse of myself in the mirror behind the bar. My one saving grace this evening is that I look good.

And I really do. This dress hugs my body in a way that is making every man, woman and magician look my way.

Morrigan catches me checking myself out and rolls her eyes at me.

I sneer at her. "What? Some of us take pride in our appearance." Slowly and with every ounce of poison I have in my body, I drag my eyes down her mundane black outfit.

Her mouth puckers. "Do you have to be such a bitch?"

"Maybe keep your judgemental eyes to yourself and I won't have to be."

"Girls, for the love of my sanity," Mother hisses.

"Your Majesty," Lord Mosel says as he walks past.

"Your Grace." Mother nods and turns back to her friends.

As he moves past me, I stiffen. He was one of the Roman associates I tried to negotiate a deal with. He could well be the one sending me death threats.

He grips my arm and moves me to the side. His fingers are so tight it makes my eyes water. Morrigan, bless her sisterly soul, catches the movement and flicks her fingers, bending and contorting them while they hang at her side.

Mosel coughs, lets go of my arm and bends forward, his face blotching red.

I rub my wrist, unable to meet Morrigan's eyes. Reluctantly, through gritted teeth I mumble, "Thanks."

My decrepit bodyguard appears, too late to be of use.

"It's fine," I say and shove past him.

He flusters, useless and dithering, and proceeds to retreat back to the wall. He does, at least, follow my movements as I stride through the bar.

It stings having to thank Morrigan. But what makes my stomach curl and froth is the fact I can't defend myself with magic like her. I'm a fucking princess for god's sake we're supposed to be powerful. It's degrading.

Lavinia—a girl I'd rather not know—shoves past me.

"Watch it," I say.

"Watch yourself, Penelope. I haven't forgotten what you did."

"Get over it already."

She leans into my face, "I was in love with him, and you fucked him. And for what purpose? You could have anyone you wanted, you're a fucking princess, and instead you went for someone taken. What was it? Spite? Boredom? Revenge for me stealing your fucking homework in year six?"

"Don't flatter yourself, Lavinia. I don't think enough of you to bother with revenge."

Her eyes bug wide, and she shakes her head at me. "You really are just as much of a bitch as everyone makes out you to be."

"And your boyfriend is a womanising whore. He offered himself on a plate, and I had an itch to scratch. What can I say, still itching, so you can keep him."

"Itching from chlamydia, no doubt."

I huff out a snide laugh. "You're pathetic."

"And you're a bitter, lonely whore. But we all have our crosses to bear."

There's a guy glaring at her from the edge of the room with the kind of possessive stare that a lion gives its prey.

"I'd be careful leaving your new boyfriend for too long, you never know when a bitter, lonely whore will find themselves in need of entertainment."

She flushes red and her hand whips out and slaps me across the cheek. My bodyguard, late once again, lurches forward and grips Lavinia by the wrists, hauling her back.

Before I can go after her and kick her in the vag—and this time definitely for spite—the door opens and standing in the frame is a group of vampires.

The bar quiets. Despite the fact Mother primed everyone, the shock—along with the silence—is absolute.

No one moves.

It's as if the entire place was flash frozen. Or perhaps, we have become the stilled vampires. This is ridiculous, they're just people like us. Albeit gross ones that drink blood and fuck like savages—rather hot, orgasm-inducing ones. But how can I explain I know that?

I'm going to have to break the ice.

I strut up to the group and scan their faces. Octavia I

recognise because of who she is. Red too. I've seen her with Morrigan's friends. The others I don't recognise. Two men, and...

Oh. Fuck.

My entire body freezes as our eyes lock.

Fuckety, actual fucking fuck with a giant, demon-sized mega fuck on the side.

There's a moment where the earth opens up and swallows me whole. Adrenaline zips around my gut and into my limbs making everything tingle. The blood well and truly drains from my face into both my feet—and thoroughly unhelpfully, my pussy.

Dahlia.

Please don't remember me. Please don't remember me. Please, for the love of my sanity, don't fucking remember me.

Her eyes narrow... and then widen.

She remembers me.

Oh my gods, I am so fucked. I am the forget-the-death-threats-Daria-and-Mother-will-just-execute-me-anyway kind of fucked.

Play it cool.

That's what I'm going to do.

Play it real fucking arctic levels of cool and hope that she realises the political minefield she'd unleash if she blurts out that I snuck into Sangui *illegally*.

Her eyes glimmer, her lips curl into a smirk that could shatter hearts, and I swear I'm going to be sick.

Bile claws up my throat; I swallow, and it definitely tastes of acid. Oh gods. I'm not laying down and giving up. I take a deep breath and pray that Dahlia has an ounce of political nous. Enough to recognise that she needs to keep her mouth shut.

I thrust my palm out, fingers tingling, and focus on

Octavia. "Lady Beaumont, the pleasure is mine, Princess Penelope Lee."

I'm kind of impressed with myself when I don't flinch as her cool fingers slide into mine. I move to her girlfriend. "Red, nice to see you again."

We shake hands. She isn't vampire exactly. Her skin is warmer than Octavia's, but she doesn't feel human either. Morrigan did explain that she's a dhampir or something. Whatever that is. Her bleached blonde hair is shaved underneath and all shaggy on top. I like it, though I think she could do with a fresh buzz.

I move to the tall suave one, a little too clean shaven and pretty for me. I prefer my partners rugged and demanding and a little dirty round the edges. Though I'd probably climb him like a tree if I were drunk.

"Xavier," he says. I shake his hand and move to the next.

"Gabriel. A pleasure," he says, tucking a book under his arm to shake my hand.

"The pleasure is all mine."

He smiles before pulling another book from his back pocket. Last, Dahlia. I swallow what feels like a ball of iron. My whole body stiffens. What if she says something? What if—

"Princess..." she says in a tone that screams of knowing exactly why she's calling me that instead of Penelope.

I'm so screwed.

She slips her hand into mine, squeezing a little too tightly, and then tugs me in suddenly.

Her mouth brushes my skin as she places a kiss on one flaming hot cheek followed by the other.

Where her lips graze my ear, she whispers. "Oh my, we have been a naughty princess, haven't we?"

I'm dead.

Literally, actually, fully fucking factually dead. I might as well stake myself, for fuck's sake.

I snap my hand out of hers, stepping back. And do you know what that motherfucker does? She smiles at me, broad and grinning. All pearly white teeth and charm. Like there's nothing to see here.

Her grin is as striking this evening as it was in the nightclub. Her entire physique is made up of lines and angles and curves. But not soft ones. She's hard and steel like. As if she were carved out of centuries of war and strife and battle. Her clothes are tighter tonight, everything clings to the curve and bulge of muscle. She wears her combat trousers, vest top and leather jacket in a way that reminds me of just how toned her body is.

I lick my lips. It's automatic. My body is about a thousand degrees. Why is it so hot in here?

I've only ever had one other woman have this effect on me. I never told anyone about us. We dated for a few incredible weeks, and then her parents left the city for work. I was only twenty and she didn't have a job, so she went with them. I was devastated. That was years ago, though. I thought it was a phase.

Clearly fucking not.

Dahlia grips my wrist. It's strong, protective. Her eyes graze my skin in a way that makes me shiver, as if she's peeling away my secrets and lies.

Mother reanimates, as does the rest of the bar. She flutters behind me, corralling us into the main area. But Dahlia keeps hold of me, her hand slipping to my hand. My eyes drop to the pulsing electricity between our palms.

"Who did you piss off?" Dahlia breathes.

"W-what?" I stammer, mentally slapping myself to get

a grip. She hasn't told anyone yet. If she were going to, she wouldn't have whispered.

"Your cheek. There's a stunning, vicious handprint."

"Oh. It's fine." I pull my hand out of hers and brush my dress down.

"I'm not sure hitting a princess is fine."

A nervous laugh stutters out. Did I just giggle? Mother of gods, what is wrong with me?

"It's lovely to meet you anyway," I say.

"Meet me... *again*, you mean?" Dahlia drops her voice.

Flames flush my entire body. Okay, we're done.

I tug her to the side of the bar, away from any prying ears.

"Please..." I say.

She quirks a single eyebrow at me, brandishing that grin like a weapon. My pussy is a traitor and it, along with Dahlia, can go fuck themselves.

Dahlia smirks. "I'm rather fond of a woman begging me. But I'd love to put a princess on her knees. See what else that pretty little mouth of yours can do," she says, her tone oozing enough confidence my nipples harden.

She must take the heat in my cheeks for anger because she laughs and licks her lips. "Don't worry, *Penelope*, your escapee antics are safe with me."

I sag in relief.

She shrugs. "Besides, I'd rather be fucking a hot woman and drowning in Sangui Cupa than wasting my time winding you up."

What the hell? What a bastard. She drags her eyes up and down my body.

"But I can't seem to find any hot women, and politics says I have to follow my sister."

That lying fucking cow. She wanted me in the Whisper Club and we both know it. My eyes flash at her crass confession and not-so-subtle insult. Something shifts; my mind wanders back to the club, and the way she was so clearly a dom. I'll bet she's butt hurt. Probably wants to punish me with a bit of degradation. My clit throbs, my skin pimples with gooseflesh.

She tilts her head at me. "What was that?" she asks.

"What was what?"

"I'm asking you. Your heart rate increased, blood is pooling beneath your skin and—"

Her eyes drop to my crotch.

My mouth parts, a little sharp breath escaping. How dare she stand there and read me like this. I grit my teeth and lean into her, lowering my voice to barely above a whisper.

"You tell anyone you saw me in Sangui City, and I'll make your life a living hell." I draw back and give her my own sinister little smile. I can play bitch with the best of them.

She chuckles. "Oh, Princess. We both know you have way more to lose in this situation than me. There's no need to be a brat about it."

But that's the thing: I am a brat, and she fucking knows it.

She shoves past me and follows after Octavia. I am left entirely flustered, unsure whether she was rude, a tease or a flirt. Maybe all three? What an arsehole. I can't work out if I hate her or if I'm attracted to her.

My bodyguard approaches. "Ma'am, I must ask if there are any other people I should be concerned about? It seems there are a couple of people in here who have taken issue with you," he says. I glance at his name tag on his jacket.

There are so many guards in the palace at the moment I can never distinguish one from another.

I snort. "Well, Marcus, I'd be hard pressed to find someone in here who doesn't have some kind of beef with me. Haven't you heard? My speciality is pissing everyone off." He gives me sad eyes, and I want to nut him. "I don't need your pity."

I march off into the bar, only to come face to face with Blane—my ex. Really? Can I not get a break tonight?

"What do you want? And how the hell did you get in here, anyway?" I say, zero patience left in me.

"You owe me a carriage."

"No. You were the one who lost it in a bet. That's nothing to do with me."

He leans toward my face. "Only because you insisted I play."

This time, Marcus appears and shoves him back.

Blane is one of those clean-cut, overly groomed men. No wonder we were doomed to failure. Not my type at all.

I shove a hand on my hip. "I didn't force you. Our choices are our own."

I stroll away until he says, "It's not like you can't afford it. Just take it from the royal coffers, for fuck's sake."

There's nothing I hate more than being used for the crown's purse strings.

I turn to face him. "Maybe if you stopped sucking off daddy just to access your trust fund and, oh, I don't know, got a fucking job, you'd be able to afford your own carriage instead of trying to bleed me dry."

"Bitch."

I smile and step away. He must lunge for me because there's a scuffle and clunking sound and then the echo of him shouting as he's escorted off the premises.

Tonight is testing my patience to the limits. I know I've had a few issues with people recently, but, for once, I'm actually trying to behave for Mother and Morrigan. It feels like gang-up-on-Pen night.

I reach the edge of the bar and take two glasses of champagne off the closest server's plate. I neck one. The fizz makes my throat sting and my tummy bloat. I swallow down a belch and sip the second glass in a far more lady-like manner.

Mother is with Morrigan and the vampires in the middle of the room at the central table. Gabriel seems more interested in whatever he's reading than what's going on around us. Though I notice that he's sat himself next to Lady Antonia's son, who is obscenely intelligent. And, it seems, sporadically engaging Gabriel in conversation.

Red, Octavia and Xavier are all chattering away with Mother and Morrigan. Dahlia, though, I can't see. I scan the room until I spot her at the bar, drinking and talking to Carmen, a girl with a figure to die for.

My stomach hardens, heat pooling in my belly as I glare at the two of them. Mother, Morrigan and the vampires are all politely laughing at each other.

Dahlia catches my eye, all while smiling, nodding and laughing at Carmen. My gaze darkens. Dahlia laughs again and then locks eyes with me. Does she think I was checking her out?

I wasn't.

And even if I did think she was hot, it's not like I would actually go anywhere near a vampire. The Whisper Club was a onetime mistake. No. I need to stick with the last thousand years of history. Vampires are all parasites. Besides, I'm perfectly happy standing here drinking cham-pagne on my own.

I'm not even lonely.

Though, I will say that night feels like a million years long.

Marcus staggers back inside, having—I assume—dumped Blane outside.

He scans the room searching for me, spots me, and makes his way over. But en route, he stumbles into a chair, followed by shoulder barging some distantly related cousin of mine.

Something is very wrong.

The guard's skin is glazed, grey and sweaty looking. Maybe Blane put up a fight. I hope Marcus knocked the crap out of him, it's less than Blane deserves.

Marcus staggers forward, leaning on the nearest table.

Yeah, he really doesn't look good. I push off the wall and down the rest of my champagne, slinging the empty glass onto a passing server's tray.

Dahlia glances my way; something in my expression must grab her attention. She jerks off the bar stool, cutting Carmen off mid-sentence and marches towards me as I head for the bodyguard.

"Princess, Penel—" Marcus says, but his words catch in his throat.

"What's wrong?" My words fall away as his skin turns a dark shade of purple. *What in the—*

"Oh, dear," he says and buckles forward.

There's a presence at my side. I turn expecting Mother or maybe Morrigan, given she did assist me with Mosel earlier. But they're still engaged in chatter a table away. To my surprise it's Dahlia, her expression furrowed as she scans the guard.

"First you insult me, and now you come to my rescue? Real charmer you are..." I say.

Dahlia opens her mouth to respond, but Marcus lurches forward. A groan that sounds like a garbled scream rips from his chest, followed by several splatters of blood.

Blood. There's a vampire stood next to me.

"Shit." I glance at Dahlia, edging away from her. Her nose flares. A shimmer of rouge flickers across her expression, and I swear she stops breathing.

"Are you going to—" I ask.

She gives a curt shake of her head. "I'm fed."

Marcus bellows out a curdled cry silencing the entire bar almost as aggressively as when the vampires walked in. I reach forward to help him up, but Dahlia grabs my hand.

"Don't," she says right as Marcus explodes.

When I say he explodes, I mean he literally eviscerates into a million pieces. Blood, organs, bone and tissue spray across the bar splattering over Mother, Morrigan, every lord, lady and royal-adjacent person in here.

There isn't even a shred of uniform left.

I flinch as I'm showered in his residue. I wipe my mouth, shuddering as it does nothing to remove the blood from my lips. My clothes are drenched in entrails, sinew and bone shards.

There's a split second of silence that stretches and stretches as collective realisation drifts through the bar. And then it's carnage.

Screams rip from one side of the bar to the next. Mine included. I lean forward and throw the entire contents of my stomach up, including—sadly—both glasses of champagne.

Dahlia slips her cool fingers through mine and drags me, running and shoving people out of the way, out the door.

"Penelope!" Mother screams, but Dahlia's grip is akin to steel clamps, and all I can do is look back at her and try not to join in the screaming.

CHAPTER 5
DAHLIA

My siblings stare at me from across the carriage, all of their noses scrunched up like I fell in a cesspit instead of having magician viscera on me. I need a shower.

Honestly, don't even know what possessed me to talk to Penelope in the first place. I should have shaken her hand and pretended I didn't remember her.

Maybe it was delusional loyalty to Octavia to make sure the 'political tensions' are eased by the end of the trip.

Alright fine, it was definitely to wind Penelope up. When I saw her image on the sheet Octavia handed out, I couldn't believe it. It took me a second to place her face. It was those piercing blue eyes that sold it. The way she stared at me from across the Whisper Club. Grinding up against me, kissing me like the only thing she dreamt of was fucking me. She wanted a piece of me, and then she left. Too chicken shit to come and take it. Well, now I understand why. Can you imagine if she—a magician princess—were caught fucking a vampire? Now that would screw the political tensions.

But I have a feeling Penelope is doing an excellent job of that as it is. New Imperium might not realise it, but they have a deviant princess in their midst, and she has been a bad, bad girl.

At least now I understand why I found her in the Whisper Club staring at Roman being drunk to death.

One little secret, one little escape. But it could cause untold damage. I press my lips together, knowing I have to be better than that. Mother of Blood, being nice is tiring. Octavia owes me, and I won't let her forget it. My generosity only goes so far.

I stare out the window as we're taken across the city to the palace. My mind flits back to our entrance this evening and the fallout after that guard exploded.

Penelope trembling outside the bar.

My hand gripping her hip, pulling her into my arms until she stopped shivering. "You're okay. You're okay."

She gave it the big balls when she first met me, but then when the shit hit the fan, she crumpled into my arms.

I shift in my carriage seat, trying to convince myself I didn't enjoy taking care of her.

But I did. Gods damned damsels in distress. Brings out my masc complex. Gotta take care of my girl. Not that she's mine. I don't even want her. I'd take any magician pussy—*yeah, that's it.* It's just about sampling a different delicacy while I'm here.

Queen Calandra came storming out of the bar, glancing between me and Penelope. I released the princess and handed her to the queen, who could tell she was still very shaken.

"Thank you," she said before a swarm of royal bodyguards smashed into me.

"Stop!" Calandra bellowed. She pushed through the

group of guards and held a hand down to me. "She was helping Penelope. Where are your manners?" Her cheeks turned pink. "Where's your carriage, Dahlia?"

I pointed to the street corner.

"Go, please. Gather your family and come to the palace. It's important we welcome you properly. This is not how I wanted the evening to go, but we must deal with this."

"I understand," I say as Octavia, Xavier and Red trickle out of the bar, Gabriel slacking behind as usual.

We left the magicians to clean up and took the long route to New Imperium's palace.

The carriage travels down the palace's long and winding driveway. Even from a distance, the building is predictably grand. But what did I expect, we're heading towards a royal castle. The road is tree lined, filled with leaves and budding flowers I can make out even in the darkness. Which reminds me, the magicians are wild over that flower thing they use here. What was it called? Sanoto? Sany? Sanatio? Something like that. They use it as a healing medicine. I think it works a lot like our natural vampire healing — pretty universal save a beheading or fatal stake to the heart.

Octavia sits rigid in her seat, no doubt pissed about what happened and paranoid about whether we will be blamed.

Xavier is lolling like he's stoned on one side of her. I'm not sure whether that's boredom or he's actually stoned. Both are equally viable. Red glances between all of us; her shoulders are tight, she feels the tension as much as I do. And it is so thick, I could drink it like an O+ breakfast shake.

Wish I'd drunk another girl before we left Sangui City.

"What the hell happened in there tonight?" Octavia says, breaking the silence.

"Someone had a bone to pick with that princess, I imagine. She had a handprint on her cheek when I walked in," I say.

"I do love a bit of drama," Xavier says, reanimating—not stoned then.

"Especially when it's not our family drama," Gabriel adds.

Octavia huffs at us. "Best behaviour when we reach the palace." She looks at each of us. Gabriel shoves a middle finger up at her from between the pages of his book.

I smirk. But Octavia snaps her gaze at me.

"What? Chill out. I drank like at least one and a half women before we left. And frankly, I've probably inhaled half that princess's bodyguard. I'm fine, aside from needing a shower." I give her an exaggerated shrug as if I don't know exactly what she's worried about.

Octavia's expression tightens. "Need I remind you that this trip is—"

I hold my hand up. "You don't, as it happens. I was winding you up, but it seems you lost your sense of humour about one long, palatial driveway ago."

Red's lips quirk and it takes a feat of fucking colossal strength for me to stifle the laugh tickling the back of my throat. Octavia really isn't in the mood. But she's such an easy wind-up.

I sigh to myself. Fighting with her is my favourite past time. "Octavia, come on. I literally went to that blonde piece of ass's rescue. It's not exactly my normal mode of operation, is it? Frankly, I'd rather have bent her over the bar and fucked her into oblivion. But—"

Octavia's mouth drops open, a simmering flicker under her gaze.

I waft a hand at her. "Best behaviour. I got it."

She presses her lips thin but seems to recognise the truth in my words. It really isn't like me to rescue some random chick. There's just something about that princess, like that night in the Whisper Club. But I won't be telling my siblings that.

I'd put money on the fact that Penelope is one of those girls who wears a mask. She makes out like she's all hard and bitchy on the outside when really, she's a quivering wreck on the inside—or in my arms. High-maintenance game player. That's what she is.

If nothing else, Octavia should recognise I meant it when I said I'd behave. She asked us to help smooth the political tensions between our cities, and Octavia doesn't ask for help lightly. I'll be good not just for her, but Red too, given she's my boss.

To be fair, she has mediated things between Octavia and me over the last few weeks, and dare I say, we're all getting along for the first time in centuries. Hell, maybe ever.

It's weird. It makes me want to stab things. I much prefer when we're discordant, at least the arguing is fun.

Maybe I will 'accidentally' spill the princess's secret and fuck some shit up at the wedding—you know, just for entertainment value.

Octavia's expression turns to a glower, as if she can read my mind.

Perhaps not.

The carriage draws to a halt, the door opening to a fresh evening, warmth glimmering beneath the air. And the thick tang of metal. Penelope made it back then.

We're stood outside an extraordinary building, though there's a distinct lack of gargoyles on the doors. I glance at Octavia. Her shoulders are tight, her back ramrod straight.

Xavier slips out of the carriage and stiffens. "I smell—"

"Blood?" Gabriel breathes.

"It's me…" I say. "Or maybe Penelope is inside. She was caked in it, too."

"When did everyone last eat?" Octavia hisses.

There's a resounding chorus of "Today" and her shoulders loosen.

"Can everyone keep it together?" she asks.

When everyone nods, she climbs the palace steps up to an enormous arched door. We trail after her, a gaggle of monsters in amongst dainty magicians. It's been a thousand years since we've mixed like this, and sure, it's only us four—well, four and a half if you count Red now that she drinks blood—and we're old enough and controlled enough not to eat our way through New Imperium.

But still.

This is going to be quite the write up, given how this evening started. The guard at the front door of the palace hesitates, his gaze flicking between the five of us and pausing on me. His Adam's apple bobs when he swallows deep, then he takes his life in his hands and lowers his gaze, head and torso in a deep and thoroughly welcoming bow. I won't lie. My eyes flit straight to his carotid, my tongue skittering out. I scold myself silently. It's the scent of iron, all tangy and rich in the air. Get it together, Dahlia.

He pulls the door open, and a fucking cacophony erupts. Red sidles inside, but Octavia's arm shoots out, slamming into my chest like a concrete rod, blocking my way.

"Mother of Blood, Octavia," I snap, giving her a little shove and rubbing my chest. But when I take in the scene, I realise why she stopped us.

"What the f—" Xavier starts, but Octavia stomps her heel on his toe. His jaw flexes.

We stare inside the door, giving each other surreptitious glances. Stood before us, are the cluster of royals still covered in blood, all screaming at each other.

There's a female guard, though she looks more like she'll kill you than protect you. I think I recognise her. She's the one that fought with us in Octavia's club when we were attacked by a load of demons. Scarlett? Yeah, her. She's stood at the side kneading her temples, looking rather frustrated.

The stench of blood is glorious. Or it would be if I could lick it off the rather delectable selection of women in front of me.

I take them in properly. The queen has curves for days. She also holds an air of authority that screams 'I'm about to fuck shit up.' She's a MILF and a half, and sadly I realise, not someone I can charm the pants off. Her hair, despite having a smattering of red splatters, is blonde like Penelope's and coiffed into an elegant up-do. Her natural olive skin makes her hair seem lighter than it is.

Penelope, though, is drenched in blood, her pretty pink dress a rather gruesome shade of claret. She definitely took the brunt of the explosion. But everyone has splatters, blood stains and the odd chunk of flesh clinging to them. Honestly, they're covered in so much blood it looks like a fresh-turned vampire's wet dream.

Even poor Morrigan's blunt-cut fringe is covered in goop. She's the one getting married according to Octavia's lectures en route. Her skin is smothered in ink and tattoos alongside the blood. Those tattoos are what make her so impressive, so Octavia said. Each one represents a different type of magic she's mastered.

Octavia made us memorise the royals' names, history and a bunch of other stuff en route, but I lost all of my fucks halfway through. So I'm patchy at best.

The screaming intensifies. Scarlett looks furious enough to take her sword and end everyone's suffering.

Penelope shrieks at Morrigan... ahh, my deviant little princess.

Well, not *mine,* mine.

The sight of her all bloody and pissed off makes my pussy clench.

Her and Morrigan are right up in each other's faces. I don't understand how two sisters can be so similar and leagues apart all at once.

Penelope's hair is as blonde as Morrigan's is dark. She has legs for about eighteen days and I'd like to bend them around me while I take her for the fucking ride of her life. Morrigan, though, is shorter. Penelope is a palette of pink whereas Morrigan is all midnight. Yet, the way they bark at each other, the two of them sharing the bluest eyes filled with fury, oh you can tell they're a vicious pair.

Penelope's eyes dart to mine. Baby blues that scream 'fuck with me and I'll ruin you.'

My stomach tightens, my cunt soaking my boxers. Maybe my siblings were right, and I do want a woman who's a living nightmare.

What kills me about Penelope though, is that no one else sees through her bullshit to what's really under her sultry gaze. She might project bitch vibes, but to me, her entire being screams 'please love me.'

Gods, she's practically begging to be broken and put back together.

Penelope holds my gaze, my body heating under the intensity "Thank you," she mouths at me.

I give her a nod, not really sure whether she means thanks for getting her out of the bar, hugging her until she stopped trembling, or keeping her escape antics quiet. Probably all three. My eyes roam her body, stripping her clothing away piece by piece.

Octavia must be staring at me, because the heat of a thousand suns burns into my cheek.

"What?" I growl at her.

"Stop gawping, she's the princess," Octavia whispers quiet enough under the shouting that she can't be heard by anyone other than our group.

"I gathered."

Scarlett catches sight of us and stops kneading her headache away, raising her hands. "Enough," she booms. And the gaggle of women fall silent.

"Scarlett Grey," Octavia says.

Which is when everyone turns to the door.

"Octavia," Scarlett says and launches away from the group to step into the doorway and, I shit you not, fistbump my sister.

Fistbump?

I rub my eyes, but no, I definitely just saw Octavia, stuffy, rigid—okay maybe I'm being hard on her, but only because Red banged the pompous out of her—fistbump another person.

If my jaw wasn't already on the floor because of the hot, deviant princess, it would be from this display of utter normalcy.

Octavia, normal? Who would've thought?

The realisation hits me that Octavia actually has friends now. I give Gabriel the side eye, and he gives me a knowing look. Glad it's not just me.

Scarlett opens her arms. "Welcome, come in. Your

Majesty, I believe you met earlier, but this is Octavia Beaumont."

The queen braces herself, like she's forgotten that I literally protected her daughter this evening.

"Queen Calandra, I assure you, we are all fed and are decidedly old, you shouldn't fear us. If there were going to be an incident, it would have been after the bodyguard's unfortunate... ah... Well, we are here with open hearts and minds hoping to solidify our recent talks," Octavia says and then steps through the doorway. She bristles as she walks, as do both Xavier and Gabriel. I step inside and realise why they all shivered.

A strange sort of pressure washes over my body, almost like the door is tickling me. It rushes from my head, into my mouth and dances around my fangs. I let out a giggle as it drops from my fangs down under my arms and around my body. A sweet, fresh scent fills the air like cinnamon and static and the hint of fresh mint. "Bizarre," I breathe.

Scarlett smiles. "The palace is just saying hello. Dahlia, if I remember?"

"The house is sentient?"

She shrugs. "Not exactly. But it definitely has personality. Nice to see you again." She holds out her hand and I take it, my eyes falling back to the deviant princess behind her.

Scarlett follows my gaze and introduces us. "I assume you met earlier this evening, but for the sake of formalities... This is Her Majesty, Queen Calandra. The princesses, Their Royal Highnesses, Morrigan and Penelope."

My eyes stick on Penelope, and the realisation that she's a princess. I mean, I *knew* it when Octavia gave us the rundown on the way here. I knew it in the bar this evening.

But hearing someone else say it. Realising I've mentally undressed a princess, *kissed* a princess... now I *know* it.

The foyer we're stood in is grand as fuck. All pillars and sweeping staircases, twinkling chandeliers that must weigh a fucking tonne with the amount of crystal hanging from them. Serene statues and gawdy artwork line the walls. The floor is a mosaic of chequered tiles peppered with the odd intricately designed one.

Scarlett drags my attention back to her as she cycles through each of us. Gabriel deigns to nod at the royal party, and Xavier executes a charming bow just as a cluster of guards come charging down the foyer to surround the queen and her family.

Mother of Blood, are we not over this? They invited us here, for fuck's sake. The guards stare at us, but the queen shakes her head.

One of the guards steps forward. "Palace has been triple checked, the carriages weren't followed. The perimeter is clear. You're safe."

A tall woman with a face like a knife pushes past the group, opens her mouth to speak to the queen and then stalls as she takes in our presence.

"Oh. You're here," the woman says.

"Daria, please. They are our honoured guests. Especially after Dahlia rushed Penelope to safety," Queen Calandra says.

So she does remember my heroic efforts.

About time.

Though she looks about as pleased that we're here and that I rescued her daughter as Daria does. Which is to say, not at all.

Honestly, I think I must have had an aneurysm in the bar. Why did I bother getting involved?

My eyes slide to Penelope's legs. Right. That's exactly why I got involved. Because my brain spends ninety-eight percent of its life in my pussy.

I shift on the spot, wishing I could adjust my boxers. Daria's face tightens, but she gives the queen a nod. Not everyone is going to welcome us here instantly, but just as Octavia has sworn us to our best behaviour, it seems like the queen has done the same with her people. This is, after all, an opportunity to open trade lines and loosen city boundaries. It will benefit the trade and economy in both our cities, as Octavia has belaboured on about for endless hours.

Queen Calandra gestures at Daria. "Please send an investigation party back to the restaurant."

"Already on its way."

The queen purses her lips. "Good. I'd like you to personally visit Marcus's family, and please let them know I will invite them to the palace once the wedding is over."

Daria nods again but doesn't leave. Instead, a hardness rolls down her back.

"What is it?" Queen Calandra says.

Daria's eyes flit to our group. Queen Calandra follows her gaze and then tuts, waving a hand at us. "Honoured guests, remember, and this is hardly the welcome I was hoping to give you all."

Octavia and Xavier wave the queen off as if being exploded on was nothing.

"What exactly happened to him?" I ask, gesturing at my blood-soaked clothes. "I mean, beyond the obvious."

The princess with dark hair, Morrigan, shoots a filthy look at her sister. "What happened is that Penelope ruined my fucking pre-wedding family dinner, because instead of going to a restaurant after your arrival, we're back in the palace covered in magician."

Penelope shoves a hand on her hip and shrieks at the top of her lungs. "Fuck you, Morrigan. I hardly call having my bodyguard brutally murdered in front of me, my fault."

Annnnd the shouting we arrived to breaks out all over again.

I try to keep up.

Morrigan's screaming at Penelope because apparently, she ruins everything.

All. The. Time.

"Oh, get a grip, Morrigan. Just because you're the heir, you don't have to be so fucking entitled. Everything always has to be perfect for Morrigan." Penelope waggles her fingers in a tone that is aggressively sarcastic.

Calandra jumps in. "I hardly think throwing childish jibes at each other is the point, is it? You're both grown wo—"

But the pair of them cut her off, bellowing savage insults at each other. I can't make out who did what. But these two make Octavia and I look like child's play. If they weren't already covered in blood, I'd be gobsmacked if their words didn't slash fatal wounds across their bodies. Scarlett, stood at the back, closes her eyes and takes a heavy breath.

It's Daria that shuts them up. "Quiet." One soft word, but it severs their argument like fangs in a throat. "We have a bigger problem."

"What is it now?" Morrigan says.

My body grows hot, not because of Morrigan, but because as I skirt around the group, I realise the blonde—I should stop calling her that, maybe legs would do instead? Princess? Deviant? Fuck toy?

I ought to stop objectifying her too. Fine, *Penelope*... has her baby blues set squarely on me. They drag down my body like she's stripping me, layer by layer, dirty girl. Only as I cock my head to watch her do I realise she's giving off the air of a very straight woman. Such a challenge. Maybe I'll toaster oven her and make her gay just for me. I mean, I am *that* good. And she did kiss me. There's hope yet.

Another woman comes sprinting down the hall. She looks the spit of Scarlett but with shorter hair.

"What the hell happened?" she says.

"Oh gods, Stirling," Morrigan says and flings herself at the woman. Stirling glances at Scarlett, they share a series of expressions that reek of Gabriel and me.

Twins.

I'd bet money on it with communication like that.

Stirling kisses Morrigan, smearing the blood away before sliding her arm around her waist and tugging her in tight.

"You were saying, Daria," Queen Calandra says.

Daria takes a deep breath. "Given the severity of the situation, and the fact that the wedding is in just under two days, all of our guards are otherwise engaged. With the investigation, the forward planning for the wedding, manning the gates, providing cover for Morrigan and yourself, we are stretched to capacity."

"And?" Penelope says, throwing that dramatic hand on her hip again.

"And therefore, I am out of guards. There's no one left to protect Penelope, and given the events of this evening, I find that to be of critical importance. Someone clearly has it out for her. We can't afford to have her wandering the palace unguarded."

The princess's pert little nose flares, just enough to spark an overwhelming urge within me to sit on it. Naked.

Penelope huffs. "I am here, you know. You can speak directly to me, *Daria*."

Daria slowly turns to face Penelope. The pair of them stare at each other for one very long second. It's the most potent silence I've ever witnessed. Penelope opens her mouth right as Queen Calandra says, "What do you suggest, Daria?"

Daria's façade cracks, the tiniest of fissures in her sharp features. As if she's been taken to the precipice of a cliff only to realise she's afraid of heights.

Her shoulders give an almost imperceptible sag. "I... I don't actually know. I'd already reached out to all my contractors because of the wedding, and they've sent all the men they can spare. I even asked some of my fae assassin contacts, but they're all busy."

"What are you saying?" Calandra says, her eyes skittish.

"We're on our own and at full capacity." I almost feel sorry for Daria. For a woman so hard, she seems almost broken, as if she's never known failure. Finally, she looks up, but directly at Stirling. One by one, each of the magicians turn to Stirling too, their expressions expectant.

Stirling shrugs. "I always know a girl. Of course I do. What about Lana?"

Daria shakes her head. "Perimeter duty."

Stirling pouts. "Jackson is excellent."

Daria nods confirmation of the excellent. "They are, but they're on royal guest duties."

Stirling pouts, scratches her chin and tries again. "Harlon Lexville?"

Daria audibly sighs. "Taken down with flu yesterday afternoon."

Rouge climbs up Stirling's neck, as she visibly searches for another name. "I mean…" she laughs, nervous and twitchy. "I always know a girl. Of course I do…"

"Well, do you think you could share it with us?" Daria says, checking her watch.

Ooft, savage. Gabriel was right, watching someone else's family drama is rather fun. Stirling swallows hard, and if I had a single ounce of fucks to give, I might feel sorry for her, but I'm a sadistic arsehole and take great pleasure in watching her squirm.

She pulls up suddenly. "Wait. I do know a girl. Or at least, Octavia… didn't you say—"

Stirling turns to me.

I frown, glance at Octavia, then to Stirling, whose eyes have narrowed at me. They're glimmering in the way a vampire's do right before they sink their teeth in for a kill.

I take a step back. "Why are you looking at me like that?"

Octavia's eyes widen as a grin pulls across her mouth. "Mmm yes, good idea," she says, nodding at me.

"Whatever it is, the answer is no," I say.

But Octavia is already nodding like an aggressive puppy at Stirling. "Yes, yes, of course. I mean, she did save Penelope tonight…"

I hold my palm up to stop proceedings. "I hardly call dragging a reluctant princess outside, *saving*," I say while staring at my sister with the most intense *What the fuck?* face I can muster. But then I remember she's not Gabriel and doesn't actually read my mind.

I lower my voice to quiet enough only my siblings can hear and try not to move my lips. "You promised me a party, and I promised my best behaviour. What are you doing?"

Octavia beams and flings an unwanted arm around my shoulders.

"She would be delighted and of course, she was head of the army for centuries. Has significant skills in strategic attacks and defence, trained in multiple forms of combat. You'd be honoured, wouldn't you…"

I say nothing, but peel her arm from around my neck.

"*Wouldn't you…* Dahlia?" She elbows me in the ribs.

Penelope barges into the centre of the conversation, her limbs flapping. "I'm sorry, but much as you were a dashing white knight earlier, I am not having some vampire as a bodyguard. Have you all lost your minds and forgotten the last millennia of hatred?" She shoves a hand on her hip.

I cock my head at her. There's those brat vibes again. Heat pools between my legs. What I'd give to bend her over my knee and make her beg for another slap.

No.

Dammit, I can't be dealing with a woman like that. I'm here to have fun. Not babysit a ball ache.

I dig in. "Good, because I'm not inclined to guard a spoilt brat of a princess anyway."

Octavia, Xavier, Stirling and Gabriel all suck in a breath.

Penelope staggers a few steps away like I slapped her. Her brows shoot up. *Wasn't expecting that were you, little brat?* I'll bet no one has ever spoken back to her. Put her in her place. This is the problem with spoilt rich kids. No discipline. No order or structure or rules. She's just a feral fucking princess.

She glowers at me like she wants to yank my fangs out. I stare just as hard, knowing I'd rather enjoy digging those fangs into her cheeks—and not the ones on her face. But I won't because Octavia owes me for behaving. I swear it's about time we found the bar, I heard this place is dripping with Sangui Cupa.

The silence is so thick it could drown a bag of kittens. No one moves until Morrigan snorts out loud like a small pig. She bends double and bursts out laughing. "Oh my god, please, Mother. They're simply perfect for each other."

I smile, smug, nodding agreement.

Until her words repeat in my mind, and the smile falls rather rapidly off my face.

Wait. What? No.

The nod turns to a virulent shake.

To my utter horror, Queen Calandra cracks a smile, the drying blood flaking off as she tries and fails to suppress a laugh.

"What is happening?" Penelope shrieks.

Morrigan—now crying with laughter—wipes the tears away. "This might just make up for the dinner. Goodnight, Mama. I'm going to get showered."

With that, she drags Stirling off, and two guards follow after them.

Calandra, hesitant, steps forward and takes my hand.

"I need an oath, if you will. I know it's unconventional, and as much as she's a pain in my royal arse, I adore my daughter. Both of my daughters. And, well, you *are* a vampire. So. If you'll excuse me, while I can see that you're physically qualified..."

She tentatively pats my bicep.

Pats it.

Fully flat palmed, like I'm a fucking dog.

What in the ever-loving fuck is happening here?

Calandra steps back. "I do require some level of guarantee."

I glance from Octavia to the queen, my expression

screaming 'help me'. Gabriel would have read it, but he's not so subtly using his book to cover his mouth, which, I suspect, is laughing in time with the bounce of his shoulders. Prick.

It's Xavier that comes to my rescue.

"Your Majesty," he starts, that familiar silk gliding through his tone.

"Xavier," Octavia growls.

Xavier clears his throat, takes the compulsion out of his voice and tries again.

"Your Majesty. We are here to begin peace negotiations. What good would it do for us to take on the role of bodyguards only to allow harm to come to your daughter? I fear that may spell the end of any relationship our kinds could have with each other for yet another millennium."

"Well said," Octavia says, clapping him on the arm.

Scarlett interjects this time. "I've fought beside them all. Well. Maybe not the bookworm. But Octavia, Xavier and Dahlia, in particular, are exceptionally talented in the art of war. I vouch for her."

I have to fight off succumbing to the compliment because, of course, I am exceptionally talented at war.

BUT NO.

What a fucking traitor. That's the last time I save my siblings or Scarlett from a demon in a nightclub. Octavia shrugs that bloody arm around my shoulder again. I crane my head up to check whether she's lost her fucking mind. I attempt to knock her off, but she holds me in place with her vampire grip. "You have my personal assurance that Dahlia will guard Penelope with her life. Won't you?"

I open my mouth, ready to spit poison on her.

"Won't you, *Dahlia*?" she urges.

Gabriel, Red and Xavier all huddle around me like I'm being presented as a prize.

Sacrificed, more like.

Octavia lowers her voice to vampire quiet. "Please, Dahlia, I need this. It will solidify our partnership and bring a new era of peace in. I'll owe you..."

That makes my ears prick up.

"Owe me what?" I whisper.

"Whatever it takes."

I take in her expression. Oh, for the love of blood, she's got that sincere, soft look in her eyes. In all the years I've known her, I don't think she's a) made such a request, or b) left the reward so open.

I slump against her.

"You owe me *big*," I say through gritted teeth.

The queen inclines her head, takes my hand and shakes it once. "New Imperium thanks you for your service."

It's the princess that ends the conversation. "Mother. Fucker," she shrieks and storms off down the hallway.

Oh, I am going to enjoy this.

CHAPTER 6
PENELOPE

I don't need to look behind me to know she's following. Of course she is. Not only is she now my bodyguard, but the vampires are here to impress Mother. I don't care if Dahlia potentially stopped me from being eviscerated this evening. I don't need a bodyguard, and I am very done being dictated to. Fuck having a babysitter, let alone a blood-sucking one. The fact she's one of only two women I've ever wanted to sit on the face of, and she didn't tell everyone I snuck into Sangui City unguarded, unaccompanied and rubbed Roman's face in it, is beside the point.

I storm into my room and slam the door behind me, hoping she gets the message.

She doesn't.

I flop on my bed, only to realise I'm still covered in blood and organ residue and stifle a scream. Gods, this was a designer dress too. I sit up as Dahlia lets herself in and proceeds to waltz around my room, picking shit up like she owns the place.

"Excuse me, your job is to stand there and make sure I don't die. Not touch my shit."

She smiles, full-fanged, at me.

"Is that supposed to scare me?" I snap, over the antics already.

There's a rush of air and I yelp. Suddenly she's right in my face, the fangs that were harmless twenty feet away are far sharper up close.

"My job, Brat, is head of training in the new unified army..."

I narrow my eyes at her. "Is that so, I heard you were demoted, *General*." I smirk.

She growls. I'm about to cuss her out for being a wolf instead of a vampire when I realise...

I got to her. I actually pissed her off enough I burrowed under her skin and got to her. Delicious.

I smile. Her eyes narrow. She's irritated as much as I am. That makes my smirk deepen.

Which makes her growl legit rumble out of her chest. I poke her smack in the middle of her décolletage. "You. Don't. Scare. Me."

Her eyes close. She takes a deep breath, using what I imagine is a considerable amount of strength and patience, and lets it out. The only hint of irritation is the flaring of her nostrils. Which is kind of cute. It softens some of her hard lines. I'm going to enjoy antagonising the shit out of her.

She draws her body back, wafting her hand around. "You are an inconvenience at a party I thought I was going to get drunk at. Much like the party you gate-crashed in—"

I'm up and lunging forward, my hand slamming over her lips. She startles, her arm wrapping around my waist to steady us. Her body presses against mine, warmth pooling between us despite the fact that her skin is cool under my touch. Everything about her is steel and strength. The most surprising realisation though, is that I feel safe wrapped in her grip.

"Don't. No one needs to know. I got in and came back. I didn't cause any trouble. So just leave it, please…"

"Sth eww do knnow ow tt ehave," she says against my palm.

"What?" I say, my face scrunching as I try to understand her words. She reaches up and peels my fingers from her lips.

"I said, so you do know how to behave. Seeing as you said please so nicely, consider your secret kept. Now, as for the rest of your antics—"

Hold on. Who the hell is she speaking to?

"Antics? Don't act like you're so much older than me, you're not my mother."

Her head rocks back as a laugh spills from her belly.

"Mother of Blood, Penelope… I'm over five hundred years old."

That promptly shuts me up. I pout. Which serves to make her laugh harder.

Whatever.

She must have been turned around the same age as me though, because she looks the same sort of age. How do you even tell how old a vampire is?

She stops laughing and turns serious.

"I think we need to have a little chat about your behaviour…"

"My—? Ugh. One, don't patronise me. And two, the only thing we need to chat about is how you're going to sit in the corner and stay quiet while I get through my sister's wedding."

Dahlia raises a perfectly trimmed eyebrow at me. "More

like you can play nice and behave yourself like the good little princess you are, or we can do this the hard way. I'll let you decide. Hmm?" She leans into my neck and inhales one, long, deep sniff. No warmth ripples from her skin and yet her presence fills the atmosphere. She's heavy, domineering, like she owns every ounce of air she passes through.

The space between my legs heats.

She lets a little gasp of air out. "Fuck, I forgot how much you smell like crack."

I shift, trying to move my underwear.

"Even with the crusted blood of some other bodyguard on me?" I say, my nose crinkling.

"I've never smelt a magician. You're divine. Fresh and sweet, like spring flowers and the deep heart of evergreen forests."

Heat rushes to my cheeks, my pussy. My nipples harden.

"Gods," Dahlia says. "You're making the scent stronger. It must be the magician's blood in you. I've never drunk one either."

That makes the heat cease. Like fuck is she drinking me. Never. Doesn't matter how good the orgasm looked in the Whisper Club. What if she can't stop. Besides, doesn't she realise who I am? How dare she assume she can just drink a princess.

I refuse to flinch. Refuse to back down. I'm not going to let some fucking lowlife vampire intimidate me. My hands find their way to Dahlia's chest, and I shove her out of my personal space.

But she goes solid and immobile. My teeth bare, the prickle of irritation clawing through my veins.

She's cool, I can feel that even through her combat fatigues.

Our eyes lock, we're close enough to kiss.

To bite.

To drink.

"Touch me again, vampire, and I'll stake you before you can swallow," I snarl.

"I like you angry," she says.

My eyes narrow. "Trying little vampire, aren't you?"

"Feisty little magician, aren't *you?*" She huffs a laugh out but steps out of my personal space. Her fingers brush her chest as if the shadow of my hand remains there.

"My name is Dahlia, try using it. Things will go a lot smoother for you."

"Well, *Dahlia,* if you don't mind, I'm going to shower off the dregs of my last bodyguard. And get some beauty sleep, given I have to attend yet another of my sister's wedding façades in the morning."

Dahlia steps back all dramatic. "Oh, I see, you're butt hurt because you're not the heir..."

I suck in a breath, my eyes bugging wide. That fucking bitch.

I straighten up, my fists balled, the pink in my cheeks flaring to crimson. "How fucking dare you."

"And yet... I'm not wrong..."

I don't care if she is a vampire and could snap my neck in a blink, I poke my finger in her chest. Hard.

"You know nothing. About me, Morrigan, or fucking magicians. So how about you shut the fuck up."

I march past her as fast as I can, my eyes stinging with unshed tears. But I'll be damned if I let her know that. I slam the bathroom door shut so hard my towel falls off the back of it onto the tiles.

She's wrong. She is. I know it.

Sure, I have had my fallings out with Morrigan, and I

know what I am: *the spare*. Doesn't mean Dahlia needs to rub it in my face. It's not that I even want to be the heir, or queen one day. Gods, I don't. I can't think of anything worse than having to deal with all the political meetings and contracts and negotiation after negotiation. I used to sit in the council meetings, once upon a time. Even tried to handle a few things.

Tried again when I was with Roman and look where that got me.

I get in the shower and rinse the majority of the gunk off me, then shut it off and move to the bath instead. I pop the plug in, letting it fill deep.

I sink under the water, the warm suds cleaning the evening away. Fatigue edges through my muscles. Dahlia's words play over and over again.

She doesn't understand.

The door flings open and a naked Dahlia strides in.

"What the fuck is wrong with you?" I shout.

"Shower. You're not the only one covered in dead magician."

"Gods." I avert my eyes while she showers off. But I find myself glancing to the steamed-up shower, wishing I could see more.

She gets out and pinches one of the towels. The door clicks shut and then rattles, a soft scratching sound like a body is sliding down it.

"You should know I don't apologise often. But... For what it's worth, I'm sorry." Dahlia's voice trails in.

My lips purse, every ounce of me wants to bite back. To remind her the only thing she needs to do is fuck off. But it doesn't matter what I say. Mother and Daria have decided she's going to be my bodyguard, and there's not a lot I can do about it.

"I'll take your silence as acceptance of my apology," Dahlia says, and I'm instantly riled up.

"Must you make everything difficult?" I say, slapping the surface of the water.

There's a muffled laugh. "I get it, okay? I know what you're going through."

I snort. Loud, indignant and firm. "Give over."

The door clicks open. She doesn't come in, but angles herself, making her voice clearer.

"You're not the only one who lives in the shadow of their sister."

I open my mouth to fight back, to shout at her to get the hell out, but I rehear her words. My brows cinch together. I'd be happier bickering.

"Fine, I'm listening."

She sighs. I can just about make out her wet hair draped against the doorframe, all wavy and thick. I wonder what it would feel like to run my hands through it. Her shoulders are bare, the towel tucked tight under her armpits.

I stare at her, lean forward out of the bath, moving this way and that to sneak a glimpse at pieces of her. Dahlia's jaw is chiselled, a little masculine, but in the way that makes a woman appear powerful.

My clit gives a pulse. I shift in the bath, pushing the heat and thoughts of her soft tresses out of my mind.

Dahlia takes a drawn-out breath, sighing it out as if the words are heavy on her tongue. "My sister, Octavia... she's one of the original three vampires. Do you know what that means?"

I retrace my memory and the conversations Mother had with us before they arrived. "That she created one of the three vampire lines?"

Dahlia nods against the frame. "In our city, that is

everything. Power. Status. Wealth. Respect. It doesn't matter that I'm one of the oldest living vampires, Octavia will always be better."

I chew my lip. Dahlia twists her head, her gaze meeting mine through the slit of the door.

I recoil, not because I'm naked, but because it's the first time I've seen softness in her. It's the way her eyes curve; they're distant and filled with something I can't quite place. Maybe she doesn't want to share it yet. I lean against the bath, giving her privacy.

Morrigan always said I was shallow because I was only interested in fashion and people. But I'm interested in people because I care. And what's wrong with fashion? How is that any different to her obsession with books? At least I wasn't standoffish and lonely. Dahlia's sharing something difficult, and I'm giving her the space to do that —how is that anything but kindness?

"The godsdamnest thing is, Octavia was hated." She hits her head against the frame, not hard, but enough for me to hear the clatter of frustration. "Our entire city feared her, and yet she loved them anyway. Can you imagine fighting for a city that resented you? For ten centuries, she battled against perception and judgement. Always thinking she wasn't good enough."

"But you knew she was?" I whisper.

"I had to live knowing that it didn't matter how old I got, she would always be older, stronger, more powerful. It didn't matter how hated she was, everyone was always more interested in her. And the worst bit of it was, she was everything: kind, strong, loyal. In spite of it all. Do you know how inadequate that makes a person feel?"

I knead the palm of my hand. I thought Dahlia was bullshitting when she said she got it. But everything she's

said is the truth of Morrigan too. Duty bound, self-sacrific-
ing, loyal, strong. Would I do those things? Be that way if I
were in her shoes?

My stomach grows heavy. Probably not.

"Yeah, I do know..." My words are so soft they're barely
above a whisper, but she'll hear them. I swear I read somewhere that vampires have excellent hearing.

"We used to fight, Octavia and me. It was vicious too,
what with us being vampires. Blood was drawn. Bones
were broken. And then something shifted. We were forced
to fight together. Don't get me wrong, I still tried to win the
city in the trials, I wouldn't be me unless I'd tried to claim it
as mine. But I was living in denial thinking I could beat her.
Besides, she was always meant to rule Sangui. I guess I'm
meant for something else..."

"And you're okay with that? When you wanted the city
just as much as she did?" I say, sitting up, trying to reconcile
how she could just quit like that.

"No. But I'm more than okay with our new relationship,
with the fact that for the first time in five centuries, I feel
like my family don't hate me. We're more than bickering
and competition now."

"Mmm." Is that enough for me? Having Morrigan as a
sister, loving each other?

She shifts, her spine lifting off the doorframe. "You
know what really changed things?"

"Go on..."

"Discovering that all along, Octavia never felt like she
was enough. That while I was spending my energy fighting
her, she was fighting herself harder than I or the city could.
If all you and Morrigan do is fight, you might be missing
how she really feels."

Dahlia is silent a moment and then adds, "Just because

you're not the heir, doesn't mean you have nothing to offer."

That sentence is a blade. It slices through my ribcage, severing every vein, artery and capillary in my body.

My eyes sting, my chest tightens and my throat swells shut. It's like she's cut me open and wrenched my insides out.

"Ugh," I groan, and sink under the water.

I hate Dahlia even more.

CHAPTER 7

DAHLIA

I don't know why I told her that. I'm not sure I've ever admitted it out loud. Not even to Octavia. Sure, we've reconciled and Red was a huge part of that. But to actually confess, to say the words out loud, that I was jealous, insecure. That I felt overshadowed by everything she was, even when she was at her lowest?

My stomach knots, heavy like an anchor. I don't do guilt or remorse, haven't got time for it. I unfurl the tangle of emotions and shove it away. The fact I admitted the truth to a total stranger concerns me more.

"Thanks," she says, her voice flitting in from the bathroom. But my body is hot, and I don't want to talk to her anymore. I want to get away, to crawl inside my skin and bleach the words out from under my gums. What kind of fucking voodoo magician is she to pry truths from me?

I wander around her room, tightening my towel. I'll need to get my case and clothes from the carriage. She has so many nooks and crannies I can't help but poke, opening drawers and wardrobes just to have a nosy.

"I guess you're right," she says, and she must be

washing because the water tinkles and splashes. "I just didn't want to admit it."

I let her talk to herself while I scour away the ugly pieces of me. My fingers brush a pile of papers and magazines on her desk. Mostly fashion, some Daily Imperium newspapers.

I knock a load off and halt. Beneath the newspapers are a pile of letters that make my fingers tingle. Written in red ink, with large flowing letters are page after page of death threats, each one more twisted and sicker than the next. Some threatening physical violence, others threaten her belongings, the palace, her reputation. The last one my fingers stumble upon makes my hands tingle.

Rape. Torture. Forced pregnancy.

What kind of sick fuck writes this shit?

I scrunch up the papers, lobbing them in the bin and march to the bathroom.

I punch the door open; it slams against the wall.

"What the fuck?" Penelope shrieks and yanks the curtain across the bath. "I'm naked. How dare you come in? Again!"

It takes an unnatural amount of strength not to roll my eyes. "You have the same anatomy as I do, and after the threats I just found on your desk, I don't give a fuck what you're wearing, I'm no longer leaving your side. Period."

"Get out of the bathroom!" she shrieks.

"Have you read those letters? There could be a predator lurking in here."

She screams in frustration. "The only predator in here is you, Dahlia."

"*I'm* the fucking predator?" I yank open the curtain and eyeball her. I have to bite the inside of my lip to stay focused on her face. Especially when every cell in my body is begging me to be a dirty perve and drag my eyes downward.

I don't.

Gods, I've grown. Look at how mature I am now.

But I am also a lowly, blood-hungry vampire, so what I say instead isn't much better. "I'm only a predator if you want your pussy eaten."

And then my eyes roll down her body anyway.

Oh well, the thought was there.

I devour every inch of her skin. Sweet Mother of fucking Blood. She is perfection incarnate. Her legs appear even longer in the water. Her neat little pussy shaved bald glimmers under the rippling water.

I swallow hard.

She flushes dark, then pink blossoms on her cheeks.

Her skin is paler than mine. I spend most of my nights outside training hunters and vampires, so I guess the moon glow has turned me ruddy. I can tell she's pasty normally, but she holds the afterglow of sun, like bees hold pollen.

My eyes wander over her smooth stomach. She's actually on the skinny side; I prefer my women with soft stomachs and too much breast to suck. Penelope's the kind of lean and athletic that would turn a sports girl green with hate. Her breasts are small, and pert. One perfect mouthful.

I swallow again.

"See something you like?" she says in a lilting tone that screams temptress.

I tut and lean down into the bath. She doesn't flinch at my nearness, but her nostrils flare a touch. Good, at least I'm getting to her.

"You know, this bitchy little front doesn't work with me, Penelope. It's all because you're too scared to let anyone in."

Her gaze turns acid, eyes narrowing at me. I expect a comeback. Some jab or jibe at me.

But to my fucking shock, she opens her legs and displays her little pink lips.

"Oh, I'll let in whoever I want," she purrs.

Three things happen simultaneously:

1. She smirks. My jaw tightens.

Followed by,

2. My pussy gets wet. Like really fucking wet.

And,

3. Every ounce of dominance screams to the surface as I decide I am absolutely teaching her a lesson, because Mother of fucking Blood does this brat need one.

I tear my eyes from the fury-inducing smirk she's wearing and examine her glorious pussy glimmering under the dappled water.

This is going to hurt me more than it hurts her, but I can't help it. It's against my nature to let a woman behave like this. I lower my hand. Tentative at first, I'll be respectful, even if she isn't. My fingers hover above her knee. Enough warmth radiates from her skin it heats the pads of my fingers. She makes no move to stop me. In fact, she widens her legs, spreading herself until I can see her opening just beneath the water.

Tempting.

Teasing.

She has no idea who she's dealing with. I'm going to enjoy the hell out of this.

I glide lower, down her thigh and stop right before her pussy. Her mouth parts like she's desperate, gagging for me to spread her folds and finger fuck her in the bath.

I smile, moderately irked by the fact I can't stop my fangs from behaving like a teenage boy in the girls changing room. They drop unbidden because all my focus is on not sliding into her cunt.

"Do you always get what you want, Princess?" I say, my voice dropping to a rumble.

She sucks in her bottom lip, her long blonde eyelashes fluttering at me as she nods.

I am going to fucking ruin you. I smile harder.

"Mmm, and what is it that you want?" I say.

She opens her legs wider, hoisting her clit just above the water line. My mouth waters so much I have to press my lips shut and swallow. I brush my fingers down her centre, she inhales, sharp. Her eyelids flutter shut as her pelvis tilts towards me.

I hover above her clit, my hand still as stone. Heat billows between us. When I don't make contact, her eyes snap open, widening as realisation dawns on her. She's not getting an orgasm, and I'm not going to touch her.

I pull my hand away and straighten up.

She slams her legs shut. "I'm not a fucking lesbian anyway," she snaps as she makes to get out of the bath.

But she slips on the bathtub floor. I lunge to catch her and keep her upright. She jerks her arm out of my grip. This is delicious, I've really pissed her off. I grab her towel and hold it up for her. Just. Out. Of. Reach.

Her nostrils flare as she steps out of the bath and swipes for it. But I'm faster and step farther out of her reach.

"Not a lesbian? And yet, no one opens their legs that confidently unless... Yeah... I'd put good money on the fact you've slept with a woman before."

Penelope looks away, feinting to the side, only to dart back and snatch the towel out of my grip.

Her eyes glint with the spark of a win as she wraps it around herself. That little brat.

She cocks her chin up at me. "Just one woman."

"And?"

"And nothing."

"Did you like it?"

"I don't see what relevance that has." She struts past me towards the bedroom.

I sigh. Gods, she's insufferably high maintenance. "Are you incapable of giving a straight answer...?"

She opens her wardrobe, purposely not glancing at me. "It wasn't bad."

She hauls on a nighty as I choke a laugh out. "Oh, Princess. If you'd been fucked properly by a woman, you'd never go back."

Penelope's eyes slide to my hands before she drags them up my body, ice leaking into her gaze as her lip curls. "And what? You think some vampire trash like you is the perfect woman for the job?"

Heat surges through me. I abandon my towel and I'm across the room, grabbing her hands and wrenching them behind her back, before she blinks. I bend her over my knee and take a seat on the edge of her bed in one smooth movement.

I lower my voice to a sinister whisper. "When you lie, the muscle in your neck twitches, and the blood rushes to that pretty little mouth of yours. You want to fuck me as much as you want the next designer dress."

She bleats out a frustrated yelp, struggling against my grip. I couldn't be more smug if I tried.

"Take your fucking hands off me," she yelps and wriggles, her bra-less tits rubbing over my thighs beneath the nighty.

Gods. If I had a dick, it would be painfully swollen right now. What is this woman doing to me?

"Now you listen to me. I've tamed many a brat over the years. If I have to deal with you for the next forty-eight hours, you're going to be on your best behaviour. Which means no more insults. No more whining. And only straight answers."

"Or what?"

Seriously? I shake my head, bemused at the fact she's still pushing. "Or..." I lean over her body, pressing her torso against my thighs and whisper into her ear. "...there will be consequences."

I shove both her wrists into one hand and tug her nighty up to her waist with the other, running the flat of my palm over her arse cheek.

"You wouldn't dare," she hisses.

I smile, my fucking traitorous fangs descending again as I grin at her. "Fuck around and find out, Princess."

Penelope straightens against my grip in that defiant way that says *try me*.

Oh, I will.

I pull my hand back and slap her still damp arse. She cries out, aghast.

"How fucking d—"

I spank her again. The scream turns to a moan, her hips tilting to angle her backside towards me.

I fucking knew it.

"Filthy little princess, aren't you?"

She wriggles against my grip. Her cheeks flame red, though I can't tell whether it's fury, frustration or the deep-seated need to be fucked.

I'm betting all three.

It's exactly how a brat should be feeling after that outburst.

"Spread your legs, Princess. I need to examine the effects of my work."

Her jaw clamps shut so hard her teeth make that godsawful grinding sound. She glares at me with the kind of fury that makes my pussy clench but dutifully spreads her legs just wide enough I can see the glisten of wet pooling at her core. She tips her chin at me, defiant. Pissy. Annoyed that she liked it. Desperate for more.

I let out a satisfied sigh. "I knew you just needed to be treated right, and you'd toe the line."

"The only line I'll be toeing is the blade drawing across your neck as Mother executes you for touching me."

I rub my hand over her arse cheek, soothing the sting. "The more you fight, the more I'll enjoy it."

I let my hand glide over her skin and between her thighs. Her breathing increases, blood flowing into her cunt, her cheeks. All of it making the air smell like that heady concoction of clean wind, sweet budding flowers and the piney heart of a forest.

She's panting, her hips grinding into my legs, desperate. My fingers reach her pussy and stop.

"Dahlia..." she whines.

"Such a juxtaposition, aren't you?"

She frowns.

"Cussing me out with that filthy mouth of yours, and yet, your pussy is telling a very different story. You're begging for it."

"Fuck you," she spits. And yet, she doesn't pull away, but instead shuffles her arse closer, giving me better access.

I slide a single finger from her clit to her soaking entrance. She gasps, then it dissolves into a moan.

"The word you're looking for is, Sir. Fuck you, Sir."

I pull away.

Her eyes flash.

I relinquish her, shoving her off my thighs so she drops unceremoniously to the floor with a thunk. Her fists ball.

I stand up, examine the finger I touched her with. She stays sitting but follows my movement, watching, waiting.

If I had more self-control, I'd wipe her excitement off me. But I never claimed to be perfect, and I'd rather like to taste magician pussy. I suck her juice off my finger and have to forcibly suppress a moan of delight. Her lips part as she watches me, her expression gleaming, and I have to wonder who is playing who. Who is actually in control here?

Her flavour coats my tongue. A delicious sweetness, something a little deep and a little sharp.

I round on her. "This is how it's going to go. One, you're going to make this job easy, and you're not to leave my side until the wedding is over. Understood?"

Her jaw flexes.

"I'll take your silence as a yes. Which brings me to two. You're going to use actual words to answer my questions."

Darkness radiates into her features, and her mouth twists into the kind of snarl only a brat can pull off.

"Yes..." She draws out the word. "Sir." Her eyebrow quirks as she says it. Testing me. *Sir. Sir. Sir.* The echo soaks into my mind.

Fuck.

She must see a crack. Because the brat pounces and leaps into my personal space.

"Oh, did *Sir* like hearing some respect, mmm? Does *Sir* like it when I call her by her proper name?" She's practically vibrating against me.

Her eyes glimmer so hot I'm surprised the room isn't on fire. Vampires don't sweat and yet, the way she stares at me, the way that fucking word coils around my chest, spearing heat straight between my thighs. I'm amazed I'm not dripping.

Another fissure ruptures in my self-control. She is testing me beyond any measure of reason.

"Three, and you're going to want to listen to this one real well..."

She pops her hand over her mouth, faking shock, and drops to her knees. Sitting on her calves and looking up at me with big innocent eyes.

She places her hands in her lap, almost nadu. *Almost.* Close enough to know what she's done. Far enough away to make me understand how much of a brat she really is.

This woman... Mother of Blood.

"Three...?" She hums like she's all sweet and innocent.

"Every time you disobey me, fail to use words, or leave my side... the consequences will get more severe."

She sucks that bottom lip in, pushes her chest out until her very erect nipples show through her nighty.

"How severe... exactly?" she asks.

I squat down, run my thumb over her lips before caressing her jaw and bringing my thumb to the dip in her neck. My fingers wrap around her throat and apply just enough pressure that she knows I could snap her neck before she could beg.

Exactly where a brat should be. Beneath me. Under my control.

"Do it. Choke me. I fucking dare you... Sir."

I hesitate. Confused. I have the upper hand. She's one word away from me snapping her neck.

"Did you have me confused for a submissive little girl?" she says.

That makes me raise an eyebrow. I run my thumb through the dip between her collarbones, pressing the slightest bit of pressure on it.

"I've spent the last five centuries breaking brattier women than you, Princess."

Laughing, she tries to shake her head against my grip, but I squeeze tighter. She places her hand over mine, increasing the pressure. "However dark you think this can go, however far you think you can push me, I will push back. I don't know who you think you're dealing with. But it's *Your Royal Highness, Penelope Lee.* And I don't bend the knee."

She shunts forward, toppling me back onto the bed and then swipes for something underneath it.

A growl rips through my chest. She pounces on top of me, a wooden stake pinned to my heart. My lips curl into a demonic smile.

I yank the stake out of her grip, grab her by the arms and spin us, so she's flat on the bed with me straddling her.

I am going to fucking ruin her. "By the time I'm done with you, you'll be begging to get on your knees for me."

CHAPTER 8

PENELOPE

"Safe word?" Dahlia demands as she pins me to the bed.

I cock my head at her and grin. "Vampire trash."

"That's two words, *Penelope*," she tuts, all dramatic, playing the game. "Pay attention, or I'll put this stake somewhere that will make you consider behaving."

Who the hell is this vampire? I've never had anyone give as good as I do. She's relentless. And I am soaked—and not with sweat. Apparently, I do like being challenged. Who knew? It's not like anyone in the palace challenges me. Gods know Blane didn't. Daria might be the only exception and that's purely over security. All Mother's staff pander to whatever ridiculous requests I make, my dramatics usually swept under the carpet.

But Dahlia. She isn't taking any of my shit, and I don't think I've ever been so pissed off or aroused.

My nipples are so hard they're chafing against my night dress, and my thighs keep sticking together.

"Safe word..." Dahlia says, the warning clear in her tone. Too bad for her, I don't seem to have a line.

"Hmm, if it's not vampire trash, how about: fuck you?" I laugh as the words spill out.

She grits her teeth and flips me on to my front.

"The problem with brats is thinking they can beat their dom. You can't. Your safe word is stiletto. Say it."

"S... S...Vampire trash." A cackle tickles my tongue as I try and keep a straight face.

She hoiks my nighty up and off my body, leaving me naked on the bed, and proceeds to spank me hard enough it's going to leave a handprint. I yelp. But my body breaks out in goosebumps as the sting turns to molten pleasure.

"Say. It," she snarls.

"Fuck. You... Sir."

I swear her skin flushes, but she moves fast and brings the stake down on my backside. I shriek, try to wriggle and scramble up to rub my cheeks, but she has me pinned on my front, my arms locked behind my back. Tears well just as her hand strokes and circles my raw skin, soothing the sting of what I know is going to leave a bruise.

A mark.

She fucking marked me.

That realisation makes a little zing of pleasure pulse in my clit.

"I'm going to ask you one more time." She slides something cool and hard between my legs right to my entrance. What the fuck?

I wriggle up and away. "Is that the stake? I thought that was a joke."

"I never joke. Safe word, Princess..."

I'm panting. Short, shallow breaths as I try and move. But I'm stuck, her grip might as well be steel chains. My clit throbs so violently I know I'm going to come whether I like it or not.

How dare she treat me like this.

How dare I enjoy it.

I'm livid.

Furious with her. Even more furious with myself for enjoying it. I buck against her grip, knowing the punishment is only going to get worse.

I want it.

I need it. I want to see how far I can push her. And I won't lie, the fact she's pushing right back and standing up to me is the hottest thing I've ever experienced. I crave the fact she's putting me in my place. No one has ever been strong enough or dared to do that.

"Trash," I spit out.

She sighs audibly and brings the stake to my entrance, drawing it around my opening. Teasing, making me soak the end of it. I shiver against her, my whole body alive with electricity. Then the cool press of wood is gone. I crane my head back.

"One last time." She grins, that same expression of chaos and curiosity I saw in the Whisper Club. Only this time, it's a little more twisted, a little more sadistic. Her expression reforms into malice and maybe a little mayhem.

"Safe. Word," she says, her tone so commanding, so fucking demanding I almost break.

Almost.

I grin, all teeth and fire: I am nothing if not defiant.

I blink slowly, making sure she knows I heard and am choosing to disobey. "Trash."

She smiles. "I hoped you'd say that."

The stake moves to my arsehole.

My eyes widen. Oh fuck. The realisation that the wood is only lubricated with me, and I am not warmed up hits me hard.

I bury my head in the duvet as she pushes the stake through my ring of muscle. It's tight, but thankfully, she goes slowly. She releases my wrists, her other hand finding my pussy and circling my clit. Moving her fingers from my apex to my entrance, gliding in and out, filling me, stretching me, pushing me to the brink.

"Oh gods," I whine into the mattress. I tilt my hips, forcing the stake in deeper. She drags it out, the sensation creating a rush of tingly pleasure through my ring. One finger in my pussy becomes two, as she glides in and out of both holes. I tremble, moaning and gasping against the duvet.

"Safe word, Penelope," Dahlia hums, though at this point she knows as well as I do that I won't be giving it to her.

When my response is a muffled moan, she pulls her fingers out and slaps my ass. The reverberations run through my entire body. My nipples rub against the bed and my whole body sings with such acute pleasure I'm convinced this is how I die.

She pushes back inside me, her fingers rubbing against my G-spot as the stake moves in and out of my arse.

"Fuck, Dahlia, I'm going to..."

She moves the stake harder, faster, her fingers gliding in and out of my pussy until I'm trembling against her, waves of golden pleasure throbbing deep inside my cunt.

Then, she stops. Oh gods, no.

"Are you fucking kidding me?" I wrench around to glare at her.

"Penelope..." she tuts. "Give me what I want, and I'll give you what you need..."

She begins thrusting the stake and her fingers inside me again. In and out she moves them. In. Out. In. Out. Then slower... This time, it makes the waves of pleasure ripple through me in a rhythmic pulse so violent my entire body tightens, taking me right up to the precipice.

And then she stops. My whole body crashing back to nothing.

I scream out, frustrated. "Please, I beg."

"The safe word, Penelope," she says, her tone mute. Final.

I say nothing. She brings her hand down on my arse— hard. My skin throbs, but as soon as I cry out, she's moving again, wringing every ounce of pleasure from my body.

Pain.

Pleasure.

Tears.

Over and over, she cycles.

Pain.

Pleasure.

Tears.

My mind drifts, vanishing into euphoria as she moves in perfect rhythm. Smack, thrust, thrust, thrust. Smack, thrust, thrust, thrust.

My body trembles and shakes. I'm no longer sure whether I'm crying or screaming or dying in heaven.

"I can do this all night," she whispers into my ear. "Do you want to come?"

"Yes," I whine. "Please. Please let me."

"You know what you need to do..."

"What if I don't want one? What if there's no line you could cross that I wouldn't come hurtling over just to spite you?"

Dahlia's expression falls. "I figured you'd say that. But that is exactly why you do need a safe word."

I slump against the mattress, defeated. "Stiletto."

She resumes her thrusting, only she pulls the stake out and flips me onto my back. Then, she sinks between my legs and draws a long sweep of her tongue over my clit.

"Fuck me," I breathe.

She moans with pleasure as she laps at my soaked cunt. Her tongue glides over every inch of me, my clit, my entrance, my folds. This is what it's like to be ravished. Two fingers find their way back inside me, and I pant out her name. Stars smatter my vision. She held back my orgasm so long I swear I'm going to combust.

She laps faster: a wild animal, starved and feral, and I am the only thing that can satiate her. I grind my pussy against her face, bucking against her mouth as her other hand digs into my thigh, fighting to keep me in place. She'll bruise me. I'll wear yet another mark from her on my body.

It's that thought that pushes me over the edge.

I come apart.

Truly.

Completely.

I think I black out? Pleasure spreads everywhere. My nipples tingle, bolts of electricity shoot from my clit to my toes. A wave of rushing heat pools deep in my pussy and fires through every cell of my body until...

I'm sobbing. Giant cries cleave me in two as a wholeness settles over me that I've never experienced before.

"It's okay," a soft voice says. "It's okay."

I'm wrapped in strong arms, a duvet pulled tight around us.

"Dahlia?" I breathe.

"Don't speak yet, just stay in my arms, that was a lot." She holds me for a while, soothing and caressing me until my tears ease. Then she reaches to my side table and grabs a bottle of water.

"Here," she says and holds it up to my mouth. I'm trembling too hard to take it myself. She helps me drink and puts it back, only to cradle me all over again. I never expected a vampire could show such tenderness. Let alone one as hard as Dahlia.

She pulls the duvet around us again and holds me, twirling a lock of my hair around her fingers and stroking me until I drift to sleep in her arms. The last thought I have is that this is the first time in my life I've been entirely satiated.

CHAPTER 9
DAHLIA

Penelope is a fucking mess. She's gone and gotten herself utterly wasted, and yet still manages to look obscenely hot. After approximately eighteen million outfit changes, she finally settled on a berry-pink strappy dress that's sheer over her stomach and most of her back and short enough that if she falls over, everyone will see her pussy because the scrap of fabric masquerading as underwear covers *nothing*.

Tonight is Morrigan and Stirling's hen do. They chose to have a joint one seeing as they share a group of friends.

I pull her by the hand off the dance floor.

"I was having fun," she says.

"You're drunk."

"So?"

I tut at her. "You're drunk because you're hurting in there." I point at her chest.

"Fuck off, Dahlia, you don't know me." She smacks my finger away.

"Really? So you're not hurting? And you're fine with

feeling like you're not a part of that? You don't feel like an outsider?"

I cock my head at Morrigan's table, where her group of friends laughs and smiles and knocks back drink after drink together like family.

Her face falls.

"I told you, I know you," I say.

She folds her arms, glaring at me. "Takes one to know one. Miss my-family-don't-hate-me-anymore."

That stings. But she's not wrong. I know her because I've been where she is.

"You think you're the only one that knows anything. But you're not, Dahlia. I see your bullshit too. You're only guarding me to repair whatever shitty relationship you had with your sister. So don't try and fucking play me at the who-knows-what game. I might not be a decent magician, but I'm fucking observant," she snaps and struts back onto the dance floor grabbing the nearest magician. Some lanky prick with a beard and limbs like twigs.

For fuck's sake, really?

Her eyes lock onto mine as she grinds up and down his crotch. My blood quietly simmers, frothing and boiling, and she knows it. She picks his hand up and makes them caress her waist, her hips, her arse.

She is exhausting. She is addictive. What kind of fucked up am I that the more she fights back, the more shit she gives me, the hungrier I get for her?

She lets out a little giggle that is far too close to a moan as she gyrates on him. My teeth grind against each other. I want to snap his neck. I want to rip his throat from his shoulders and watch his life force spurt over the dance floor. Who the hell is he to touch her?

A presence looms next to me.

"Dahlia," my sister says.

"Octavia."

"That's not the whiff of jealousy I smell on the air, is it?" She follows my gaze to the princess.

"I legitimately have no idea what you're talking about. I'm here to do a job. I'm here because I have your back and nothing else."

"So you're not fucking the princess, then?"

I stiffen. Even though I'm not looking at her, I can tell she's smirking.

"So you are?"

"Obviously not. That wouldn't aide the intercity politics, would it?"

"It certainly wouldn't if you were to break a heart. And you are very good at that... need I point out the trail of women left in Sangui?"

I glare her. "She's a grown woman. Whose face she decides to sit on is entirely up to her."

"She sat on your face?"

"Octavia, dammit."

She laughs. And I punch her in the arm.

She rubs the spot I landed a blow on. "Thank you. Maybe I didn't say that clearly enough before, but I am grateful you're taking one for the team."

I shrug. "I figured five hundred years of bickering was enough."

She smiles. "And how is the bickering with little miss princess?"

"She is the most infuriating woman I've ever had to deal with."

"So you're falling in love, then?"

"Don't be ridiculous. This is just a job."

She raises an eyebrow at me and sucks her lips into her

mouth as though she's swallowed down whatever she was going to say."

"What?" I bark.

She closes her eyes and takes a deep breath. "Nothing, nothing. But for the sake of both our cities, don't hurt her. I don't want anything jeopardising the talks. This could truly be the first time in a millennium that our cities are at peace."

I turn to her, trying to hold back a shitty tone. "You think I don't know that? I just got through telling you I had your back. Hasn't everything I've done since being here demonstrated that?"

She nods and squeezes my shoulder. "It has. But sometimes what we think we're doing up here," she touches my temple, "and what we're actually doing there," she touches my heart, "are two different things. Besides, she seems like a handful."

"Yeah, well, handful is my speciality."

She gives me a solemn look and then strides off, and I relocate the princess in the crowd. She's now grinding against some other random guy, a curvaceous girl dry humping her thigh at the same time. I knead my temples, my fangs dropping. I hate that I feel possessive over her. It's not my place. Octavia is right, she's not mine. Regardless of what happened last night. This is none of my business. I'm just here to guard her.

My skin bristles. I'm not sure whether it's suppressed rage at the sight of Penelope dancing with two other people or something else.

I decide she's had quite enough fun for this evening. I make my way through the crowd. She spots me and her grin deepens. She thrusts her arse into the guy and gropes the woman in front of her. Fuck me. I am going to spank that princess so fucking hard when I get her home.

The back of my neck prickles like someone is watching me. Or maybe not me, but her. I freeze. Penelope must spot the change in my demeanour because she stops dancing. She sprints over and slides her hand into mine.

"What is it?" she breathes, her skin shining. The air fills with the scent of hot skin, endorphins and a cocktail of gods knows what brimming in her veins. It's delightful. I want to bite her. I want to fuck her. I'd quite like to drown her... or maybe drown in her. But not now.

"I'm not sure," I say and scan the club. The room is filled with dancers and party goers. "And everyone in here is a friend of Morrigan's? There're no uninvited guests?"

"As far as I know. Mother has pretty tight security. Daria nearly made Morrigan cancel the entire hen do because of the threats I'd received. But they agreed they would do a closed-door party."

My back warms. I spin around but see nothing. The air ripples. I rotate on the spot, turning, turning, turning, completing a full three-sixty of the club. But it's as though whoever or whatever is watching is always one step ahead. Always out of my line of sight.

"And the security? How good is Daria?" I breathe.

"Good." She indicates in her direction. Daria is standing like a pillar at the back of the bar. I agree—she looks as much like a knifepoint tonight as she did the first time I met her. There's a rush of wind. I grab Penelope and spin out of the way, flattening her against the wall, my body pressed against hers.

She yelps. But I stand firm so no one can get to her. But even with my vampire sight, I can see nothing out of place.

"Yure squathing ee," she mumbles into my shoulder

blade. I ease the pressure off her body and hold my hand out.

"You're coming with me," I say. "We're walking the room. Stay behind me and do not leave my side. And this isn't one of those times when it's a good idea to fuck about. Got it?"

She stares into my eyes. Something about my expression must convey how serious I am because she nods, and her grip on my hand tightens.

She slides in behind me and we walk the perimeter of the bar. Something is off and yet nothing is out of place. Only Daria standing in the corner of the bar looks like she's miserable. Everyone else is dancing or drinking. Octavia, Scarlett, Morrigan and a bunch of their friends are all sat around a booth table necking shots and enjoying the view of some half naked dancer.

There's another rush of wind and that's when I smell it.

The faintest hint of metal on the air, of cool steel and something else. It's almost as if...

"I think there's another vampire in here," I say.

"What?" Penelope gasps. Her grip on my hand tightens so much it hurts.

A figure stands by the back door. It's too far for me to see clearly, but I spot it. Male, about six-foot-two maybe taller. I can't make out any more from this distance even with vampire sight. He skulks out the door and vanishes. He doesn't move like a vampire, though. Maybe I was mistaken.

"Stay with Daria," I bark, pushing her to the other side of the bar where Daria stands. I speed through the club. She'll be fine on her own. I don't want to leave whoever the fuck that was out there free to cause trouble later. If he's the threat, maybe we can finish this debacle tonight, before the wedding starts. I'll put money on the fact Octavia would be high up in some influential magician books if we did.

I'm out the door and on the street in a flash. Thank you, vampire speed. The guards by the door startle and lunge for me, but I swat them off, and they quickly realise who I am.

But whoever that motherfucker was is long gone.

Likely swallowed by the crowd of people thronging outside the club. The people and the paparazzi. I close my eyes and inhale the night air. Try to detect the hint of vampire I got. But there's nothing other than the stench of booze, sweat and hormones—who the hell was that?

I continue searching the surrounding night, desperate to find whoever is just out of my reach. But I see nothing. He was wearing a long trench coat, but all I see are a bunch of half naked magicians in far too few clothes for how cold the night is.

Maybe it wasn't a vampire at all? Maybe it was just some overly hench magician. Penelope did mention fucking up some deal with three guys. It could well have been one of them.

I slope back inside the nightclub to find Penelope standing with Morrigan, not Daria. They look like they're having an intimate conversation. And I know all too well about those sorts of conversations between sisters. But the fact she's disobeyed me hasn't gone unnoticed. I don't want to get in the way, but also, I am self-aware enough to know I am nosy and stand close enough I can just about hear what they're saying.

Besides, I am her bodyguard. It's a legitimate need to be close enough to her so I can protect her if necessary. Especially after whoever that was lurking about just now.

Morrigan rolls her eyes at Penelope, who stiffens in response.

"Let's stop bickering for a second," Penelope says.

"I didn't start it," Morrigan snaps.

"Would you shut up a minute, I am trying to do something nice here."

Morrigan huffs in response but dutifully closes her mouth. "Sorry."

"Thank you," Penelope says. "Let me start by saying, *I'm sorry. Okay?*"

"I beg your pardon?" Morrigan steps back, her eyebrow raised at Penelope, and my heart sinks. I can tell Penelope is being genuine, and Morrigan isn't making it easy. But as soon as I recognise that, Morrigan must too because she softens and says, "Really?"

"Yeah, really." Penelope hangs her head. "It's just that I've always dreamt of having a princess wedding. You know? Like a real one with a poofy dress and all the attention on me."

Morrigan cups Penelope's hand. "You're aware you actually will have a princess wedding one day..."

Penelope shakes her head and frowns at her sister.

"First of all, you literally are a princess, Pen. So, of course, when you find the right person, you'll have the full-blown wedding of your dreams."

Penelope stands a little straighter then nods slowly. "I guess. I hadn't really thought of it like that. Anyway, I know we've had our issues, but if it was my wedding, I would want it to be perfect, and I suppose what I'm saying is that this is a peace offering, and an acknowledgement that I'm not going to do anything to fuck this up for you, okay?"

"Okay?" Morrigan says, her tone mildly disbelieving.

"Look, I don't want to make a big deal of this, but I learned about this tradition from a different city. It's where the bride has something old, something new, something borrowed and something blue. And given yours and Stirling's house, I just thought... Well, I thought that you may want these..."

She pulls a little velvet box out from her purse and hands it to her sister. Morrigan opens it and her eyes immediately well up.

"These were Nana's," Morrigan whispers, her voice all choked.

"Yeah, they were. They're old, and blue, new to you and borrowed from me. I thought maybe you would wear them. Given, I'm sure, that everything else you wear will be black, I thought they'd be a cute flash of colour."

"Oh, Pen," she says and closes the box and pulls her sister in for a hug. "They're beautiful. Are you sure you don't mind me wearing them? I know she gave them to you before she passed."

Penelope shrugs. "I'd like you to wear them, I think it fits the pair of you. Just keep them safe for me and give them back when you're done."

Morrigan nods, and I take that as my cue to go and escort Penelope out.

I sidle up to the pair of them. "Evening, Dahlia," Morrigan says.

"Good evening, I think it's time for the princess here to leave for the evening."

"Hell, no," Penelope says. "I was just getting started." She snatches her glass from the table where all Morrigan's friends sit and glugs the rest of it.

Great, so now I have to deal with an increasingly drunk and bratty princess.

Morrigan's mouth presses into a thin line as if she's trying to squash a laugh. "Now you see what I have to put up with?" She laughs.

"Exhausting." But I sling my arm around Penelope and drag her back into the crowd where no one is listening.

"Who was it?" she says as she takes my hand and ducks under it, swinging herself around me in some kind of odd pirouette.

When I'm stone-cold sober, I don't dance, and unfortunately, I'm still unnerved by whoever that figure was earlier.

"I should speak to Daria."

"Did you actually catch anyone?"

"No."

"And they're gone?"

I nod.

"Then why don't you chill out for a minute and dance with me." She shoves her arse into my crotch and gyrates on my pussy.

Fucking hell. My self-control up and dies. My fingers grip her hips as she grinds harder and harder against me. I want to slip my hand under her dress, push my fingers inside her pussy and fuck her on the dance floor.

Actually, that's not a bad idea. I spin her to face me. I pull her in tight and waltz us around the dance floor.

"The waltz? Showing your age, aren't you?"

"I'll have you know this dance is the dance of noble vampires, and you should be thankful I know how to lead."

"I'll let you lead in the bedroom too, if you like…"

My nostrils flare. She grins at me, knowing exactly what she just said. "You're drunk."

I hold her hard enough to bruise and pull her around the floor. "Need I remind you, you don't *let* me anything. Do I need to teach you a lesson?"

Her eyes glimmer with just the faintest hint of rebellion. I pull us to the heart of the room where the dance floor is thick with bodies. We're a mass of hot flesh and sticky booze. The lights are low, and everyone is drunk enough we won't get caught for what I'm about to do. The music shifts, dropping to a more rhythmic beat. Around us people couple up, spinning in slow circles. Kisses are swapped, hands caress waists, tongues push inside mouths.

I lower my voice. "How disappointed would the queen be if I finger fucked her daughter into a quivering mess at her sister's hen do?"

Penelope's lips quiver. She sucks in her bottom lip, those fucking deliciously long blonde eyelashes fluttering at me.

"I suspect the queen would be devastated if she caught me cavorting with a dirty vampire."

"Dirty? Oh, Princess, you have no idea how filthy I can be."

I wrap her arms around me and slip one hand between her legs.

When I reach the apex of her thighs, I gasp. I expected to find the scrap of underwear, but my fingers brush freshly shaved skin.

I shake my head. "When did you remove those? Do you have no decorum?"

"Maybe I was out looking for someone to fuck. Someone who could actually give me what I wanted."

My jaw ticks, I grip her tighter against me and without warning, push a finger inside her pussy. To my surprise, there's no resistance. Apparently, backchat and disobedience are foreplay for her because her pussy is more than wet and accommodating enough for me to slide a second finger inside her.

She gasps, but it dissolves into a moan as I pull my fingers in and out. In and out. In and out.

"Don't make a sound, Penelope. You wouldn't want to alert Mummy to the fact there was something wrong, would you?"

Her eyes are hooded, drugged with the pleasure of me fucking her. I lean in and whisper as I curl my fingers to find that spot on her inner wall, my palm grinding against her clit. "You wouldn't want to let Mummy find out what a slut her little princess is, being fucked in the middle of a nightclub, would you?"

"Oh gods," she moans and rocks her hips against my fingers. Her legs quiver and she wobbles, but I hold her tight against my body. I'm not going to let her go until she comes on my fingers.

"Harder," she breathes.

I go slower, dragging out the pleasure, letting my palm apply just the right amount of pressure to make her squeak.

I grin.

There is nothing more satisfying than controlling someone's pleasure.

"Please, Dahlia. Fuck. Please..."

Just when I was having fun, too. I can never resist a woman begging me. I sigh and shunt my fingers inside her, hard this time.

She moans, her head falling back. "Oh gods," she says as her walls tighten against my fingers. I pull out and shove my way back in hard and fast. Over and over. Her nipples rub against my chest, the buds tightening against the sheer fabric of her dress. What I would give to take one in my mouth and suck it until she screamed my name.

Her pussy clenches around my fingers so tight I can barely thrust them in and out to tip her over. "Relax,

Princess," I say, trying not to weave compulsion into my voice.

The hair on the back of my neck stands up again. I lose my focus, my eyes instantly scanning the room instead of fucking Penelope.

"Dahlia," she whines, "What the fuck, I'm so—"

"Quiet," I snap and pull my fingers out. I scan and check the room. There' are too many dark spots, too many corners covered and too many places someone could hide and only one fucking exit.

I'm done.

We've had enough fun in here. If Penelope were actually attacked and I didn't stop it, I can't imagine what would happen to Octavia's peace talks.

"We need to go," I say and use the hand I didn't fuck her with to drag her to the side of the room and towards the door.

Queen Calandra appears, her face a mesh of confusion. "Where are you going? The night is young."

"I am not comfortable keeping her here," I say.

"Do you have any evidence of an intruder?"

"I do not. I have my gut and my vampire instincts, and they're telling me it's time to leave."

She presses her lips together. "Most unconventional. But I suppose you are her bodyguard, and you are doing your duty to protect her. So be it."

She holds out her hand for me to shake. My eyes widen. But she's already moving closer to take my hand...

The hand that just fucked her daughter.

Mother of Blood.

As if in slow motion, Calandra slides her palm against my still sticky fingers and shakes my hand. I dare a glance at Penelope, who is now as crimson as Octavia's eyes with her lips pressed so thin I think they've vanished.

"Good evening," Calandra says and pulls her palm away, her brow crinkling ever so slightly as she looks at her hand.

Penelope drags me to the doorway. "I will never live that down," she says.

"Lucky for you, she didn't seem to notice." I bring my hand up and lick the remains of her pussy off my fingers. Which, might I add, tastes fucking divine. I can't wait to shove my face between those long legs of hers and feast all night.

Penelope turns a lovely shade of green as I laugh to myself, and we head for the exit.

CHAPTER 10

PENELOPE

My cheeks still feel like they're a thousand degrees. I was completely frozen, unsure whether I should scream at my mother to stop, or stay quiet because, let's face it, how was I going to explain to her that she couldn't shake my bodyguard's hand unless I told her why? And gods know there was no way I was going to tell her I just let a vampire finger fuck me to an almost-orgasm in the middle of Morrigan's hen do.

I'm about to open my mouth and give Dahlia a load of shit when someone knocks into me.

"Watch it, blondie... ah, Penelope, about time we had a chat..." Lord Brinkley says, but Dahlia is lightning fast and closes her hand around his throat.

"Apologise. Now," she demands.

"S... S," he tries to choke out.

"You stink of booze," Dahlia growls and shoves him away. "Pay attention."

He swallows hard, wiping his hands down his suit jacket—who wears a full-blown suit in a nightclub? He must be sweating his tits off. His hands have left filthy smear marks on me. Vile.

"Wait," I say, having an inkling of an idea. Roman never gave me any dirt to force one of their hands, but maybe if I can scare them into compliance, I can force the deal to completion and hopefully stop whichever one of these idiots is sending the letters and terrifying the palace.

I lean into Dahlia's ear. "Play along with me, will you?"

She cocks her head at me but nods her assent.

"Lord Brinkley, have you been sending me letters?"

He frowns, shaking his head.

"Are you sure about that?" The shaking turns to a nod. The fear gouging deep lines across his brows makes me think he's being genuine. So be it.

"Have you ever met a vampire?" I ask, pouring as much sweetness and light as I can into my tone.

"N-no," he says, drunk enough to slur.

"Allow me to introduce you to Dahlia St Clair, my vampire bodyguard."

His eyes are so wide, I swear they're going to pop out of his head.

"Dahlia has been in New Imperium for a couple of days now, and given they're here for very important political talks, she's been unable to eat anything. Do you know why that is, Lord Brinkley...?"

He shakes his head, his face paling.

"Because she only drinks blood. Now, you and I have some unfinished business, don't we?"

He blinks at me as his Adam's apple bobs up and down.

"Mr. Brinkley, I think you should use your words," I say, trying not to laugh as I strip him of his lordship.

"Unfinished... Right. Yes. Well, it's a big risk, none of the other players are offering to hand over the promised goods," he says, his eyes darting between Dahlia and me.

"Yes, but someone needs to go first, don't they? That's going to be you, isn't it? Mr. Brinkley?"

He makes to shake his head, but Dahlia, Gods bless her vampire soul, takes a step closer and smiles at him, full-fanged, every ounce of malice and venom I know she possesses poured into her glinting gaze.

Lord Brinkley stops shaking his head and nods very aggressively at me.

"Oh, wonderful," I say, exaggerating every word. "That's simply wonderful. Isn't it, Dahlia?"

She closes her lips over her fangs and winks at me.

"See to it that Mosel gets the fae contracts by the morning. Good evening, Lord Brinkley."

Dahlia shifts forward suddenly. Brinkley about shits himself as he jerks away, scampering back into the nightclub.

A bone-deep smile settles all the way into my belly as we head towards the exit. I finally did something useful and all by myself. I'm feeling entirely smug until Dahlia opens the door.

Then, I scream.

Mother paces back and forth up and down the now empty nightclub. It's odd being in a room painted black but with the house lights on. A bit like knowing how a magic trick is done, it spoils the illusion of the club. Mother's eyes carry a fever as she flits between me and the dead body in the middle of the dance floor.

I sit in a booth, my legs tucked under my chin, my arms

wrapped around my knees to try and stem the trembling. But it doesn't matter how tight I grip myself, my teeth still chatter, and I can't seem to get warm. I keep giving the corpse furtive glances. Every time I do, bile claws at the back of my throat.

I bury my head in my thighs. The flashing memory of Dahlia unhooking the woman from the doorway keeps replaying over and over.

She was hanging by her neck, her head limp and lolling to the side. But that wasn't what made my skin crawl. It was the fact she was dressed to look like me: long blonde wig, short pink dress, a face full of makeup. They even put blue contacts in the woman's eyes.

Gods, it was the way she stared out at nothing. I shiver.

Maybe it wasn't Brinkley, Mosel or Jeremiah fucking with me. Brinkley was here tonight, after all, and after the warning we gave him and how terrified he looked, I really doubt he'd have the balls to kill a girl. I mean, it could have been one of the other two. But who the hell else could it be? Bane isn't capable of murder; he's a useless prick at the best of times. But then, he seemed desperate enough to harass me the other night. And as for Lavinia, I always thought her more of a queen bee bitch. But what if I pushed her too far? I did sleep with her boyfriend. Maybe she's trying to terrify me out of pure revenge, a kind of public humiliation at the most crucial of royal events. I wouldn't put public humiliation past her, but murder? I trawl my memory trying to come up with anything else I may have done to Lavinia or her family that might have pushed her over the edge.

Whoever it is that has a problem with me, they are escalating. They fucking killed a girl, for gods' sake.

Dahlia shucks her jacket off and slings it around my shoulders.

"Here," she says and strokes my leg. The movement is slow and measured. Despite the cool touch of her skin, a warming comfort swirls through my limbs, and after a couple of minutes, my nervous system responds and the trembling ceases.

"Thank you," I say, and she slides her hand into mine, squeezing.

Morrigan's friends are huddled around her. She's super pale and keeps glancing at me. Octavia and Scarlett chat in quiet tones a little way off. They occasionally point at the body and then cover their mouths as they discuss what I assume is strategy.

Dahlia doesn't leave my side. She's tense, her entire body rigid and on high alert. Taut lines of muscle strain her neck as she scans and rescans the room.

"It's okay," I whisper.

"Nothing about this is okay, Penelope. I have a job to do. What if that had been you?"

"Is that all I am? A job?" I hiss.

Her jaw flexes. "That's not... I didn't mean it like that. But clearly this threat is real."

The nightclub door slams open, making us all jump. Dahlia leaps in front of me, her arms out wide, only to see Mother's head of security, Daria, storm in and halt when she sees the body.

Her eyes drag across the room until she finds me, still living, still breathing.

Her lips purse. "What the fuck happened?"

"We don't know," Mother says, sidling up to Morrigan. "Morrigan, you should head home. You need to get out of the city and back into the safety of the palace. I'll send Pen after you."

Morrigan nods and then approaches me as she weaves

her way through the club. When she reaches me, she just stares, blinking and examining my face.

She takes my hand. "It wasn't your fault. Whoever did this is sick."

I nod. We are so rarely kind to each other that on top of everything that's happened and how tightly wound my body is, my eyes well up.

"Okay," I manage, but my voice is small.

"I know we fight, but I don't know what I'd do if that was you. I'm so grateful you're okay. Can I... Umm. I'd like to hug you."

Tears finally spill over, but I am already untangling myself and shuffling along the booth seat to wrap myself in her arms.

"Fuck, Pen," she breathes into my neck. "Thank god it wasn't you."

I whimper into her embrace as she rubs my back, letting me cry.

"Daria and her team won't let this go. You know that she'll investigate thoroughly. We'll be okay."

"I'm not letting this go either," Dahlia says. "Nor is she being allowed out of my sight."

"And for that I'm grateful," Morrigan says, giving Dahlia a polite smile. Her eyes flit between us, a small furrow between her brows. But she doesn't say anything before heading out. Her group of friends follow after her, as does Mother. Only Daria, Octavia, Dahlia and me remain.

"Come on, I want to examine the body." Dahlia tugs me out of the booth and towards the corpse. She leaves me a couple of feet away when my fingers tighten so hard around her grip that I think I might pop a knuckle out.

She kneels by the body, tilts the head this way and that, and then picks up the arms, examining the hands and wrists. Brushing her thumb over a set of two small bruises, she glances at Octavia. Something passes between them, and Octavia's face hardens.

"Any thoughts?" Daria says.

Octavia glances at Dahlia but neither of them offers anything. "I should be leaving," Octavia says and strides off to find the rest of their group.

"Really? Nothing?" Daria says, her tone as sharp as her expression.

Dahlia purses her lips and stands. "She wasn't killed here. She was brought here after the fact. Are there any security guards you can question? See if they saw anyone milling around or looking suspicious this evening?"

Daria folds her arms. "They're being questioned as we speak. Is there anyone who might want to hurt you?"

I shrug. "Sure, loads of people, but pissed enough to actually murder me? I'm not sure. I think I'm more of an irritant than anything."

Dahlia, the wench, nods in agreement. I want to tell her to fuck off but her eyes curl in delight, as if she knows she's jabbed at me. She peers at the woman's face, runs her finger along her lips and freezes. "There's something inside her mouth."

She wrenches open the jaw, a sickening crunch as the bones grind and pop under the pressure. She pulls a note out. It has a single word written in blood on it.

TOMORROW.

Daria unfolds her arms and takes the paper. Her nostrils flare. She holds it up in one hand and bends and contorts her fingers in the other. The note hovers in the air, and she makes some sweeping movements with her fingers moving in rapid patterns. The blood letters lift off the page, dissolving into a million tiny particles. They spin like a tornado and siphon down to the woman's mouth, vanishing inside.

"It's her blood," Daria says, her words heavy. "I was hoping it was someone else's, and that maybe we'd have another clue. If that's everything, I'm going to do a forensic deconstruction on her body and sweep the club for evidence. Unless you have a strong stomach, it would be best if you left."

Daria holds her hands out and begins bending and twisting her fingers. A shimmer erupts from her fingertips and blooms around the room.

"Come on, let's let her focus," Dahlia says and pulls me away. As we pass Octavia, the pair of them share that same look that sets my teeth on edge.

CHAPTER 11

DAHLIA

I'm uncomfortable. Not just because the carriage we take back to the palace is rickety as fuck as it rolls over the city cobbles, nor because Penelope is passed out in my arms and her knobbly elbow is digging into my rib.

But because there's a shift between Penelope and me. Subtle, slow but significant, nonetheless. Octavia may have been winding me up, but she wasn't too far off the mark. The close proximity and being unable to leave her side are muddying my mind too. Even though she was stood next to me when we discovered that body hanging from the club exit, my blood froze in my veins.

What's thrown me is what went through my mind.

I should have been paranoid about failing as her bodyguard, worried about the political climate and the damage this might do to Octavia.

But the only thought in my mind was: thank fuck it wasn't her.

I didn't *want* it to be her. I keep having flashbacks of the woman hanging and the frisson of pins and needles that swept through my body.

I don't want to think about what it means.

She's still asleep when we arrive back at the palace, so I carry her in my arms all the way to her bedroom. She burrows her head into my chest and makes these light snuffles that I desperately don't want to think are adorable. I like holding her like this, protecting her. Knowing that I've kept her safe.

But I'm also exhausted; a rare feeling for a vampire because we don't often sleep. I slide her into bed, taking off her dress and stripping myself of my clothes. I'll just have a sit down, maybe read while she sleeps.

Only once I'm in bed next to her, the pattern of her snores is so melodic, I find myself nodding off.

♛

I wake with something curled against me. It's soft and oddly warm. In fact, *really* warm. Why is it so hot? I peel my eyes open and hiss as a bolt of blistering pain rushes up my arm.

"Shit," I shout as long beams of afternoon light make their way across the bed. "Shit!" I scurry into the corner of the four-poster bed, wrapping myself in layers of drape fabric.

"What? WHAT?" Penelope shrieks as she jerks upright, throwing yet more of the bed drapes open. I can tell because the curtain I'm curled in warms and my skin bristles against the heat.

"Window," I shout.

"What's wrong with it?"

"Mother of Blood, Penelope. Did you forget I'm a vampire? Close the fucking curtains..."

"Ohhhh, fuck," she says.

The bed shifts and I risk a peek through the tiniest sliver of fabric. She pads softly across the carpet to the window and closes the curtains. Finally, the warm drapes cool. I untangle myself from the safety of the thick fabric.

"We must have slept most of the day away," I say. "But for future reference, unguarded light like that is enough to give me some blisters and a face lift. So, thanks." I waft a hand in the direction of the now covered window.

Penelope stands there staring at me.

"What?" I ask.

She sucks in her bottom lip, and my nipples peak. I'm suddenly very aware that I'm completely naked, and she is dragging her eyes down my body like she's licking up every last drop of pudding from the bowl.

"I just... I'm taking in the view, that's all."

"Well, it's rude to stare. So why don't you do something about it?"

She strides over to me and then stops suddenly.

"What's wrong?" I ask.

"Don't worry. It's nothing."

She slopes off towards the bathroom, but I'm not having that. She was clearly about to say something.

I fling myself over the bed and enclose her in my arms, pressing my chest to her back.

"Tell me what is going through your head." I'm not demanding or dictating, I genuinely want to know.

She wriggles out of my grip and faces me but can't seem to actually look at me. I slide my fingers over her chin and pull up until she locks her gaze on mine.

"Penelope," I breathe.

"I guess, I've had fun. That's all. And we haven't exactly talked about whatever the hell this is."

She looks at me pointedly. I don't answer because she's right. Whatever this is has become the elephant in the room. It's just... this situation. I'm protecting her while we're here and... We're... She's right, I don't know how to answer that either.

"What is... what do you..." I start, but my words fade because I don't know how to finish the sentence.

"What are we?" she asks, her eyes all doey and cute, and I want to take the stake I fucked her with and shove it right into my chest. This is just a bodyguard assignment. A favour for Octavia, nothing else. It was never going to be anything else. It's not like we could ever be anything more, we live in different cities. We're different species, for fuck's sake. She's a royal magician princess and I'm some common vampire. How could we ever be anything more than temporary?

A hard lump forms in my chest and throbs like I'm wounded and bleeding out. But it's the truth, isn't it? How would it work?

My eyes fall away from hers, my fingers loosening on her chin. I don't have an answer for her.

"I thought as much," she says, and steps out of my grip.

"Penelope, wait—" but she's turned her back on me and stepped into the bathroom, closing the door.

Fuck.

When Penelope has finished adorning her face in several coats of makeup, she does this odd movement with her fingers and knuckles and her lips change colour. If we had time, I'd love to understand how their magic works. But I'll have to learn it from a book. Maybe Gabriel can suggest something.

She glides out of the bathroom looking angelic and slips a black and two-toned blue coloured bridesmaid dress over her shoulders and turns her back to me. She's barely said more than three words since she left the shower. She's gotten dressed in sheer silence. I don't think in all the days I've been here I've ever heard her this quiet for this long.

"We should talk," I say.

"Can you zip me up, please," she says and inches her backside towards me.

I chew the inside of my cheek and dutifully tug her zip into place. She turns to face me, and my mouth hangs open. Her dress is long, the fabric smooth and satin-like. The blue swirls almost pirouette over the slight curves of her body to look like ocean waves.

"Wow," I say, the words just slipping out.

She huffs out a sad little laugh. "Thank you?"

"No, no, thank you for giving me such a glorious view... Listen," I say suddenly serious. "Earlier..."

She turns away. "It's fine."

"No. Listen. Please."

That little beat of submission gets her attention.

"Go on," she says but still can't quite bring herself to look at me.

"I would love this to be more... you are... damn, Penelope, you're everything I've ever wanted..."

"Why does it feel like there's a 'but' at the end of that sentence?" she says.

A loose lock of blonde hair falls from her up-do, so I slide it back into place, lean in and kiss her. Her lips are soft and warm. She tastes like mint and roses, her lip balm no doubt.

"Because there is a 'but,' and I think you know it as much as I do."

She lets out a breath so heavy I feel it in my lungs.

"We live in different cities," she says.

"We have different lives." I answer.

"If I wasn't a princess..."

"And if I wasn't a general..."

Thoughts whirl through her expression as she bites her lip. "It's just that this has been the best couple of days I've had in years. Even with everything that's been going on."

"Me too. I just don't see a way it can work after this. Do you?"

She shakes her head, her eyes welling. "No."

"Then let's make the most of this while we can."

What I don't say, is that she is the kind of memory I will hold for as long as the moon shines and the night runs through my veins. Because if I admit that, then this means something. *She means something.* And if that's true, then I don't know how I'll go back to Sangui City knowing the perfect woman exists, but she's out of my reach.

Her eyes soften, her fingers brush against my jaw as if buried beneath my skin is the answer. But there isn't one. We don't get a happy ever after.

I lift her up by her thighs, marching her back and pinning her against the wall.

My lips find hers. But the way she kisses me is different. It's not fuelled by lust and heat, it's slow and longing. I kiss her back, realising that everything about this aches.

Hands and mouths caress each other. Tongues slide, unfurling an aching heat in our mouths. The longer we kiss, the more my stomach knots.

I yearn to take her with me to Sangui City. But this trip is about politics, so we always had an expiration date.

Her hands curl through my hair, insistent, needy. She tugs on my scalp, driving the embrace deeper, more urgent. She grows hot beneath my fingers. I place her on a table and slide the dress over her thighs, running a finger over her lace underwear.

Her mouth grazes my neck, her teeth nipping at the skin. I hiss and pull away as my fangs descend. She grins, the devil in her eyes and demons in her heart.

"Don't play with fire, Penelope, that's how you get burnt."

"What does it feel like?"

"To drink? Or be drunk from?"

"Either? Both. I'm dying to know. When I was in the Whisper Club, I saw this woman and she..." Pink flecks her cheeks.

I pause, searching for the right words. "It feels like serenity and bliss, like molten lava and the glimmering of a thousand moons. It tastes like wildfire and winter air, like summer blooms and all the orgasms under the night sky."

"Wow," she breathes. "And for me?"

"It tastes like the biggest orgasm of your life."

Her eyes bug out at this, and I chuckle to myself.

"Bite me," she says.

But I shake my head. "Absolutely not."

She pouts at me. It is, without exception, the brattiest expression I have ever seen.

"And why not? What's wrong with my blood?" she whines

"Nothing. I would get on my knees and bleed for you, if it meant I got to taste you. But you don't heal the way I do, and I don't think marking your pretty, smooth skin right before your sister's wedding is the done thing. So how about we save that for another time."

She opens her mouth and then closes it, the realisation washing over both of us that there won't be another time.

Her eyes drop. My stomach sinks. I hate it when she looks sad. I never want to be the cause of that expression. My fingers find their way to her lace panties.

She gasps.

"You don't need me to bite you to give you the best orgasm of your life."

Her expression melts, lust pooling in her heavy eyelids. "Oh," she hums. "Then what do I need?"

"Just my tongue." I lean down between her legs, licking my way up her thigh, all teeth and lips until she rests against the wall and spreads for me.

I slide my hands over her hips and pull her underwear off. She has the prettiest pussy I've ever seen. Fuck blood, I'd rather eat this for the rest of my days.

She glistens. I should praise her, tell her what a good girl she is, but I know that won't work. I grin, knowing exactly what will have her soaking this table.

"Look how wet you are, Princess."

She sucks her bottom lip in.

"Is that all for me?"

She nods and shifts her backside closer to the edge of the dresser, spreading her pussy to obscene proportions.

"Such a dirty little whore." I wipe my finger down her slit, coating my finger in her excitement. "Open," I demand.

Her mouth drops, obedient at last. I slide my finger over her tongue. "Clean it."

She sucks my finger, drinking down her excitement. My entire body tightens at the sight of her doing exactly as I command.

It's a drug.

She's a fucking drug, addling my brain, fucking with my reality. She soaks into every cell and pore and my mind fills with her. Every muscle heats, my pussy throbs. I haven't let her touch me. Not yet. I don't often let women touch me. But I need her. Need to see her between my legs, obedient, pleasing me.

I pull my finger out and she bites down. I growl as I yank it out and she giggles.

"Oh, don't worry," she says. "I have something that will make it better."

She takes my injured finger and slides it up her thigh right to her entrance. She pushes me inside her soaking cunt. And then she rocks on my hand, fucking herself, taking exactly what she wants from me.

I'm so stunned that I've allowed her to take control. She's worked her way into my system like poison. Infecting me.

"Fuck me, Dahlia," she whispers. "Please?"

Her words are a spark and an ignition. I drop to my knees and draw my tongue over her wet slit. I lick her pussy — lapping and flicking at her hardening clit.

"Oh gods," she moans, her hips bucking. "More, please, more..." she begs.

Her words flood my mind; wave after wave of chemistry alters my brain. I want to give her more. Give her everything. I slide another finger in her pussy and she gasps. She tastes sweet and musky and like a hit from the strongest blood I've ever consumed.

I realise then, I don't want to let go. Regardless of what we said, I don't actually want this to end.

But it's going to. I fuck her slowly, lovingly. I don't go hard; I don't spank her or out-dom her brat.

I worship her.

And that is terrifying. I listen to the movement of her body, tilting my head and moving my tongue, focusing on her, her body, her pleasure. I adjust, move and wind her tighter.

Her pussy throbs against my fingers, tightening and loosening as I drive her higher and higher.

I glance up and note the hard points of her nipples against the silken fabric of her dress.

"Dahlia, fuck," she breathes.

I suck her clit into my mouth and rub against her wall. Soft, soft, hard. Over and over. Her legs shake against my cheeks, she's panting and sweating. I glance up again and realise she's crying.

I pause.

"Don't. Don't stop," she says. "I'm so close."

I lap at her pussy faster and faster, my fingers moving in a steady rhythm, dragging the pleasure out as long as I can. Her body practically vibrates against me.

She bucks twice; she's ready. I drive my fingers in hard against her wall. She gasps. My tongue flicks her clit once, twice more and she cries out. There's a rushing vibration against my fingers and then she soaks me, squirting over my face and chin as she screams my name.

I grin, thoroughly fucking pleased with myself as I lap up the remains from her still twitching pussy.

She's completely boneless and unable to communicate, so I lift her up off the dressing table to avoid any of her juices messing up her dress and carry her to the bed.

We stay there, spooning. And I think it's the most normal thing I've ever done. I lay my head on her back and close my eyes, wishing it wasn't the first or the last time it would happen.

Wondering whether it's better to have had her, knowing I have to lose her, or if I should never have come here at all.

My chest aches so hard, I'm struggling to breathe against her skin. Strange really, that we can ache for something we've never even had.

CHAPTER 12

PENELOPE

My whole life, Morrigan has been composed. She's calm and controlled. Everything, and I do mean everything, is thought through, planned and strategised down to the most minute of details. How she ended up falling for the living chaos that is Stirling, I'll never quite know. But as I open the door to her dressing room, I come to a grinding halt.

Morrigan, in her black lace wedding underwear is pacing back and forth. Up and down she strides across the room, wearing a lovely line in the carpet. The air is hot and sticky with a sweet sort of frazzle. The room is just like any other in the palace, grand, with elegant furniture, oil paintings on the walls and in this particular space, a sofa, armchairs, a bar, a dressing table and long mirrors hung on the walls—perfect for getting ready.

Morrigan aggressively twiddles her fingers, bending her thumbs and shoving them in her face and around her head. Why is she using magic to do her makeup? Her hair moves and swirls. But it's not until she turns to face me that I realise the problem.

Dahlia glances at me, her face taut as she peeks back into the room. "I think you're safe in here, maybe I'll leave you to handle this one on your own."

"Wait just a second? I may need a favour," I say and step inside. "What's going on, Morrigan?"

My sister halts turning to us. Dahlia averts her eyes from a half naked Morrigan, and I try extremely hard not to show any reaction at the state of her appearance.

It's... bad.

"I... I can't do it," she says and then flops on the floor and starts crying. Like hysterically sobbing.

What. The. Fuck? I mouth at our mother over Morrigan's head. Mother stops chewing her nail and gesticulates wildly at the back of Morrigan's head for me to do something. As if I can magically fix it, when we all know I can't *magically* fix anything.

Mother gestures more aggressively so I skooch down and kneel by Morrigan, pulling her chin up to look at me. Her skin is a mess of blotchy red, smeared mascara and daubs of various shades of eyeshadow. There must be seven different colours, none of them matching.

Gods, it's worse than I thought. Her hair, while dyed to perfection, is half in and half out of what was supposed to be her coiffed style for the day. There's a bird's nest on one side, a plait that's partially tangled and still managing to fall loose.

Morrigan's bottom lip wobbles but she finally answers my question. "Daria said there was some issue with security clearance and given all the threats, she wouldn't budge on it. I told her it's the same makeup artist that's worked on Mother for a gazillion different events. I tried begging but she put her foot down and said no."

"Okay, and how did we get to... ah, this..." I pull back and gesture at her face.

"I tried to do it myself—"

"Classic Morrigan," I huff.

She glares at me.

I wave her off. "Sorry. Not helpful. I'm an arsehole. Continue."

She pouts but says, "I tried to do it, but it didn't look right. So, I tried to fix it, but I made it worse. And then I got stressed. I tried again but the more I tried to fix it, the more my magic fritzed because..."

"Because it's a big important day and you're emotional and lost control?" I say, running my fingers through her hair.

She purses her lips and then says, "Exactly. I can always fix things." Her bottom lip wobbles, her eyes go watery. "But I can't do it. I don't have time to learn the magic."

"Do you trust me?" I ask.

Her face scrunches into a pained expression. There's a stagnant pause and then we both laugh. I get it. We've not exactly had the best sisterly relationship, have we? But on this I can help.

"I can't do what you do, Morrigan. I've never been able to harness magic the way you do. I can just about change my lipstick. I didn't master hair colouring, or those cool outfit changes you do. I had to learn everything the hard way. But it does mean I can fix this. Will you let me help? I'll even let you have my wedding present if it helps..."

She lets out a little whimper, a couple of those unshed tears spill out. "You already loaned me Nana's earrings."

"Please? I can help."

She purses her lips but finally accepts.

"Thank you."

I spring into action. "Mother, will you show Dahlia where my makeup case is? I need my hair products, curling iron and straighteners too."

Mother gathers herself up and mouths *thank you* at me as she gestures for Dahlia to follow her.

While we wait, I find Morrigan a dressing gown and help her into it so she's semi decent. Then I gather up some moisturiser I find in the cupboard along with makeup pads and a hairbrush I dig up. I sweep Morrigan into the chair in front of the dressing table and mirrors.

"What are we thinking? Chic, moody, sultry or sexy?"

Morrigan pinches her mouth together and closes her eyes. "Classically beautiful, I think. My dress is wild enough."

I dab some moisturiser on a makeup pad and wipe away the varying shades of eye shadow on her skin. The more I clear away, the smoother her face becomes, the blotches and redness fading along with her stress.

"Thank you," she whispers. "For... well, both things."

I rub her shoulder but continue my work. The problem with not using magic is it all takes so much longer and there's not a lot of time left before the ceremony.

Once her face is a blank canvas, I untwine the cluster-fuck of hair styles she's created, brushing it out until her long black locks are smooth and pin straight.

Dahlia and Mother return with my supplies just as I tug out the last knot in Morrigan's hair. Mother cracks open a bottle of fizzy Sangui Cupa, a new twist on the drink apparently. I take a sip, and it tingles the entire way down my throat. Morrigan necks her glass and then sags in her chair, a rather happier, albeit glazed look on her face.

"Thanks, I needed that," she says and burp-hiccups. I have to suppress a laugh.

Dahlia practically squeaks in the corner.

"I thought you only drank blood," Mother says.

Dahlia guffaws. "Then I guess there's a lot you don't know about vampires."

Mother hands her a glass and makes to say something but stops herself.

"Is there something you'd like to ask?" Dahlia says.

"Actually, yes..." Mother and Dahlia slip into quiet conversation, exchanging information about magicians and vampires alike.

I layer a base coat of foundation over Morrigan's skin and then get to work. Smoky eyes, a sweeping flick of eyeliner and delicious lashes. I had some spares in my case, so I lengthen hers at the corners. I add a thick gloss to her lips; Morrigan's eyes are extravagant enough, and I'm sure Stirling won't want her mouth smeared in rouge. Next is her hair. An elegant up-do ruched at the back with some curls I have to force into shape with my tongs—her hair does not like curling, and it takes practically half a can of spray, but I win eventually. They spill around the sides of her head and frame her face to perfection.

I'm done.

She looks incredible, if I do say so myself. I step to the side and both Mother and Dahlia stop what they're doing, their mouths dropping open.

"Wow," Mother says. Dahlia just blinks.

"W-wow good?" Morrigan asks.

"You did well, Penelope," Mother says, beaming at the pair of us.

Morrigan stands up, but I hold a hand over her face.

"Wait. Close your eyes," I say and then spin her around to face the mirror and wait.

"Open," I breathe.

Her expression goes stony and my stomach plummets. Oh gods, she's upset. I ruined it. She hates it.

"If you don't like it, I can change it, we still have time to—"

"How could you... you're going to make me cry."

My chest tightens, my eyes sting as my stomach falls the rest of the way through the floor. I thought she looked beautiful. Fucksake. I knew it wouldn't be good enough. Nothing ever is.

"I'm so—" I start and turn to leave, but I'm hauled back, Morrigan's arms flung around my neck as she face plants us into the sofa. All while still squeezing the life out of me.

"I look incredible. You have no idea how hard it is not to cry with gratitude," she mumbles into my neck.

"Oh!" I say relief washing through me. "Gods, Morrigan, how about start with that next time. I thought you hated it."

She shoves me in the arm before scrambling to get up. "Will you help me into my dress?"

"Of course." I smile, and she extends her hand to pull me off the sofa and leads me into the side room where her dress hangs on a mannequin.

I gasp. "Gods. It's stunning." The bulk of her dress is black. The corset has a sweetheart bustline, leaving her décolletage free of fabric. It has a layer of lace and tiny black crystals stitched into the fabric giving it a gorgeous textured effect. It cinches into a tiny waist and then poofs out into a stunning ruched skirt. Most of the skirt is black, but there are folds of fabric in two different blue colours that swoop around and meet in the middle kind of like waves.

"It means something. Between Stirling and I, that is," she says.

"The dress?" I ask, confused.

"No, the blue colours. I saw you looking at the wave-like ruches."

I nod. "It's kind of like your beach house."

She smiles, her eyes soft. "You got it."

I loosen the corset and help her step into the dress.

"This thing weighs a fucking tonne. I hope you've been working out," I moan as I lift the dress up to sit on her hips.

We shuffle to the mirror, and I can't help but let out another gasp.

She smiles at me. "Thank you for today."

"Oh, shut up. You can pay me back by making sure I have the pinkest, most girly princess wedding any girl could dream of."

She smiles. "I wouldn't expect anything less."

She wriggles into the dress, and I tug at the corset ribbons to cinch the waist in.

"Tighter, Pen."

I pull and wrench, my face turning red with the effort.

"Tighter," she whines.

"Fuck's sake, Morrigan, you need to be able to breathe too."

"Do I? Just make me look good."

"Could you sound any more like me today?"

She laughs and I do too.

"Besides, I think I already made you look perfect."

"Agreed." She smiles at me through the mirror as I put my foot in the small of her back and yank one last time.

Her eyes bulge. "Yeah, that will do," she chokes out.

I snort and have to wipe my eyes to stop the laughter

tears. I tie up the ribbon, letting the two different blue silk threads trail down her back.

"Ma, we're ready for you..." I say and our mother, our queen and our only remaining parent steps into the doorway.

She claps her hand over her mouth, tears streaming down her cheeks.

When she finally speaks, it's soft. "I wasn't the most supportive of you in this relationship at the start. But I need you to understand that I am so proud of you, Morrigan. And one day you will make a most ferocious queen. But if Stirling ever hurts you, I swear I will serve her heart up in a jar to Scarlett."

Morrigan simultaneously sniffs and coughs out a garbled laugh. "And I suspect you told her this yourself?"

Mother smiles. "Every word of it... including the apology."

Morrigan embraces Mother, who reaches out and tugs me in, smooshing the three of us together in a tight hug.

There's a clearing of a throat and then a quiet knock on the dressing room door.

"Sorry to interrupt Your Majesties, but Benedict says it's time,"Dahlia says.

"Ready?" I ask, and Morrigan nods. "Let's get you hitched."

CHAPTER 13

PENELOPE

The hallways leading up to the throne room are dark with all the windows covered in drapes. Buried in the fabric are thousands of twinkling lights that sparkle like stars. It's cute, and makes me feel like we're outside, and obviously keeps Dahlia and her family safe given it's still the afternoon.

As I watch the swish of Morrigan's puffy skirt, the ruches and wave-like fabric moving with her steps, I notice the odd sparkling gem buried in the folds. It kind of matches the twinkling in the windows. It's understated, elegant, and beautiful. Our styles differ so much, I honestly thought she would choose something wretched. Especially given my style is clearly superior to hers; at least I give a shit about my appearance. But Morrigan looks simply divine, a true bride.

We make our way through the corridors, which are lined with a deep blue plush carpet so thick it feels like my feet are sinking into the depths of ocean.

At the throne room's arched doorway, we pause. I'm to

go in first, and Mother will accompany Morrigan down the aisle.

I open the door a creak and peer inside. The hall, though already large, has been stretched. Thank you, palace. It's expanded itself enough to accommodate more than five hundred magicians and a handful of vampires.

Dahlia steps up beside me. With Father gone, I was intending to walk down the aisle alone, given Mother is walking Morrigan. But with what's happened, no one is allowing either of us out of security's sight, not even for the short walk down the aisle.

She smiles at me and holds her arm out. I slide my hand over her forearm and grin back. She looks incredible in her suit, and I won't lie, I do feel considerably safer with her by my side.

The fact Dahlia looks dapper as fuck in a suit that could have been moulded around her body helps more than somewhat. I push the thought away, knowing that today is it. She'll go back to Sangui City when tonight is over and whatever this fun was, will be done. I flick a piece of dust off one of her lapels, and she tucks a loose strand of hair behind my ear.

"Beautiful," she mouths at me. My cheeks flush.

"Huh," Mother says, looking at us. She narrows her eyes, glancing between Dahlia and me.

"What?" I say, brushing my dress down, wondering if I've spilt something on me.

But she's just staring at us. She shakes her head as if coming out of a reverie and says, "Nothing. Anyway, I've spoken to Daria. There are dozens of guards in there, camouflaged in wedding attire. If so much as a fly misbehaves, it'll be handled."

I hate that we even have to discuss security at such a

romantic time, but with the corpse last night and the threat of 'Tomorrow,' we all had to be out an hour earlier for a security briefing. Mother's just being careful, I suppose.

"Go on now, the music has started," she says.

I pull the door open and slip inside, closing it behind me. Together, Dahlia and I stroll up the aisle to the orchestral music.

All eyes stare at us, or maybe mostly at Dahlia. Of course, it doesn't matter if Mother has deemed the vampires welcome, a thousand years of hatred is hard to erase overnight. But she stands tall, her eyes set on the dais in front of us where Stirling and Scarlett stand.

Stirling rubs and pulls at her hands while she stares at the door, her focus honed on the handle.

Scarlett, wearing a suit that matches my bridesmaid dress, rubs her sister's shoulder, and Stirling relaxes, some of the stiffness easing out of her posture.

Her hair is the same as always, though it looks like she put the effort in to straighten it, her asymmetric bob pointed to perfection. She has a light coating of mascara and lip balm but nothing else. I didn't really expect her to wear a full face of makeup though, it is Stirling, after all.

Her outfit though, is exceptional. She's in a corset with the same sweetheart neckline as Morrigan's dress and matching suit trousers. Her outfit is white, but as she turns to face me, I grin. There's a swathe of fabric across the corset that spills down onto her trousers: two blue colours in a ruching wave.

I shake my head. They haven't even seen each other's outfits and they're still matching.

Wild. Those two really are meant for each other. I'm not sure whether I want to be sick or bawl my eyes out from the cuteness. Both. Definitely both. I can't stand it. I want a love like this.

"You're going to be okay," I mouth at Stirling as we reach the dais and slip into the left side to stand near our seats. She smiles at me, but it comes out a bit too much like a grimace, an odd shade of green washing over her expression. I bite the inside of my cheek so I don't laugh. Today is one day I refuse to be a bitch.

The music shifts. It's time. I'm practically giddy, hopping from foot to foot until Dahlia slips her hand into mine to make me still. There are more than a few lords and ladies whose eyes drop to where Dahlia clasps my hand. But they can shove their judgements up their arseholes. Nothing is going to ruin this day.

Finally, the music crescendos and then, the doors open and Morrigan and Mother appear.

There's a chorus of shocked oohs and ahhhs and gasped smiles. I can't help smiling so hard my jaw aches.

Stirling's mouth falls open as she gazes at her bride. I glance between them, Morrigan wears the same awed expression as Stirling.

It's a kind of mesmerised awe. Gods, it's so cute. Scarlett beams next to Stirling and subtly throws glances at Quinn—who I've just noticed is sat a few seats behind where I'm standing. Her brother and Jacob are next to her and then Remy and Bella on the other side.

When Morrigan reaches the bottom of the dais, I hop into action, lifting her skirts to enable her to climb the short steps to meet Stirling.

Mother tiptoes up to kiss Stirling's cheek and whispers something in her ear that makes a tear trail down her face. Stirling nods at Mother and kisses both her cheeks in return before facing Morrigan.

Mother leaves the dais and takes her place in the front row with the rest of Morrigan's friends.

"If I never see another sight, I'll die having gazed upon the most beautiful view in the realm," Stirling whispers, though I'm close enough to hear.

"Gods, you absolute charmer," Morrigan says, but she's giggling and blushing through the makeup.

The pair of them are grinning all toothy and wide like idiots, and it's adorable. Despite the fact there's no natural sunshine in the throne room, their smiles light up the cavernous hall.

The officiant steps up to the pair of them and clears her throat. She's an older woman, with chin-length grey hair and wearing a dark suit. The ceremony begins like any other wedding: a run through of the seriousness and sanctity of marriage, followed by the joys and possible trials they'll face.

I stand quiet, listening and reflecting. Dahlia's thumb strokes my palm. I'm not sure she realises she's doing it. I smile to myself, enjoying the way she presses a little harder at the beginning of each stroke, and then lets it soften as she sweeps out of my palm.

"The rings, please," the officiant says. Scarlett pulls two boxes from inside her suit jacket and hands them to her.

Stirling pushes her hair behind her ear and plucks Morrigan's ring from the officiant's hand. She glances at the room before taking a quivering breath and then focuses all of her attention on my sister. The way she looks at her makes me swoon. It's as though the entire world has vanished, and the only thing left is them, their rings, and their vows. Stirling stares at her as if she is the light, and the dark, the sun, the moon and all the water in all the oceans. And when Morrigan smiles, it's as though Stirling were staring upon the gods themselves.

"Wow," I breathe.

"Yeah," Dahlia whispers back, and I wonder if it's because she is thinking the same as I am. That I wish someone would love me so intensely. So obsessively and possessively that they would stare at me the way Stirling is Morrigan.

"Morrigan Lee," Stirling begins. There's only the faintest hint of a tremor in the first syllable but by the time she's finished our surname, her tone is strong and steady and then she says...

"We fucked up."

There's a moment of stunned silence and then Morrigan lets out the most unladylike pig-snort giggle I've ever heard.

Behind me, Remy cat calls, "Strong start, Stir," and the audience erupts into titters and mildly nervous laughter.

Stirling, charming as ever, turns to her guests. "Bear with me, folks."

There's a few friendly jeers and hollers, but everyone is smiling.

"I'll start again," Stirling says and clears her throat dramatically before winking at the crowd. "Morrigan Lee, we fucked up. But... I'm the lucky one. We so nearly lost each other, but the gods gifted me a second chance to win your heart... and another runic poker game."

Morrigan laughs, her eyes welling with tears. "I still maintain that I won that night. I got the grimoire..."

Stirling tuts and shakes her head at Morrigan. I have to press my lips together to avoid giggling at the pair of them. This is so typical of Stirling; three seconds in, and she's ad-libbing and off-scripting her vows.

Dahlia grins at me. She's not tearful, but then she doesn't know them the way I do. She hasn't heard the squabbling these two do over dinner when they recount how they met at some dingy runic poker club lock-in.

Dahlia tilts her head and whispers, "I'll admit, it's cute."

Stirling continues. "Hush. These are my vows, you get your turn in a minute. As I was saying, I was the winner... Not because of the poker, or the runes, but because I won you, Morrigan. You are the greatest prize of all."

Morrigan's mouth forms a little O. I have to wipe the bottom of my eyelid. Fucking romance. This is exactly why I want to get married. Gods, it's so slushy I think I'm going to pass out.

I refocus on Stirling so I don't miss a single word.

"I always thought negotiations were about winning. But rule one of any negotiation is always be willing to walk away. But that's the thing, Morrigan. I'm not willing to walk away. Not anymore. So for once in my life, I am bone deeply happy to lose. And I did... I lost my whole heart to you... willingly, openly, with my soul bared to you... I am, and always will be, on my knees for you. My love. My life. My Queen."

Morrigan's lip trembles and I don't blame her. Tears streak my cheeks, and my throat is so thick I can hardly swallow. I'm struggling not to wail like a banshee. We've had so many fights over the years, but watching her standing there, looking like a goddess, with a woman bleeding love for her, I've never been more proud of my sister. All those fights, the hurt, it all seems meaningless in the face of such ferocious love.

Stirling takes a deep breath. "Marrying you will be the greatest negotiation of my life because I vow to always compromise on whether we're spontaneous or calculated."

That earns a chuckle from the audience. Everyone knows Stirling is chaos incarnate while Morrigan is about as organised, planned and precise as you can get. Even Morrigan is laughing. I catch Mother's eye as she laughs into a tissue, her features swollen with pride as she stares on at her eldest daughter.

"I promise to challenge your overthinking and ground myself when I get too wild. I vow to stand by you through every hardship, deal, promise and negotiation. As your equal, your wife, your lover, your person. But above all, Morrigan Lee, I swear to you that no matter where you are, no matter how far from me you travel, I will always find you where blue meets blue."

That does it. Morrigan lets out a whimper, two tears fall down her cheeks and she lunges forward to plunge a kiss on Stirling's mouth.

The officiant coughs awkwardly. "A little early for that, Your Majesty," she says.

Stifled laughter ripples through the room, but everyone is smiling with those glossy wet eyes you only ever find at weddings.

Stirling slips the ring on Morrigan's hand and then it's Morrigan's turn.

"Stirling Grey. For the longest time, I thought everything I needed to know could be learned from a book."

Stirling smiles and shakes her head at her.

"But, it seems that love is the exception. Trust me, I asked a professor." She winks at Remy, and her group of friends all erupt into cheers and hollers.

Oh my gods, I'm giggling and I don't even know what their in-joke is. But it doesn't seem to matter, the whole room is joyful with them. The air is warm and buzzing with a golden energy. I thought Morrigan would read from a predefined set of vows, but between them, this is carnage, and I absolutely love it.

Morrigan continues. "You may be a negotiator, but you're also a teacher. You taught me to love, to see myself for who I am. To embrace my power." She looks down and huffs a little to herself.

"You showed me that real power isn't a crown or a title. It's the ability to let go, to live in the moment, to stop trying to control the outcome."

Stirling is incandescent as she gazes at my sister. It makes my entire body warm and gooey. Dahlia hands me a tissue, Gods know where she got it from, but I'm grateful, nonetheless. I am the definition of an ugly crier, and I am barely holding my shit together.

Morrigan squeezes Stirling's hand. "But more than anything, to be vulnerable, because I'm safe now. I know that you'll catch me, you'll save me and no matter what, you'll find me."

Stirling nods in time to all the things Morrigan says.

"Everyone thinks that I'm the most powerful magician. But they got it wrong. You are. Because you hold my whole heart. You are my equal, my better, my soulmate. You taught me what no book could. That some risks are worth taking. And I know I will take a thousand more if it means I get to keep you."

She slides the silvery band into place on Stirling's ring finger.

"I vow to go on every adventure your heart desires. I promise to have your back in every negotiation. I swear to pursue the art of spontaneity..."

There's another round of loving snickers.

"Above all, I will spend my life learning how to be your anchor, proving to you that this truly is the greatest deal you ever made because this one is meant to last forever. It's meant to last long beyond old age and skin wrinkled with love. It's meant to last even when our souls part this realm and live again in another. Because that's the thing, Lady Grey, I will spend eternity searching for you in every sunset, every horizon and every ocean wave. Until I find you where blue meets blue."

She leans up and clasps Stirling's cheeks, placing her mouth on hers. And this time, the officiant doesn't stop it. I'm pretty sure they pronounce them wife and wife, but I can't hear through the roaring cheers of all the magicians in here.

Someone chucks confetti into the air. It triggers a ricochet. Thousands of fluttering pieces of paper. The air fills with paper hearts and flowers and petals. My sister and her wife walk out of the throne room, confetti raining down on them, surrounded by the happiest hoots I've ever heard.

CHAPTER 14
DAHLIA

I'll give the magicians their credit, they don't half know how to turn a room around.

We all exited the throne room to have drinks and canapés in a side hall. But within an hour, they'd done that magical fuckery with their hands, ribbons of magic flowing from the walls, and *swoosh!* the room was completely different. I forced Penelope to stand and watch as I was fascinated. She whined until I promised I'd fuck her into oblivion one more time after the wedding was over.

The room is now dressed with chandeliers that look like cresting waves, made of blue and white frothing crystals. Tables line the perimeter with a huge black-and-white chequered dance floor in the middle. On the dais where the thrones usually sit is a long table for the royals and Stirling. Near the huge doors, Remy fiddles with a set of large boxes that pump out music.

Every guest in here is smiling and laughing and cheerful. I am none of those things.

Daria has done her best, and her security is in here. They were far more discreet in the ceremony because no one was moving. But in here, you can tell who they are because they're the only magicians not bopping their heads in time to the music. On the one hand, it's reassuring. But on the other, if I were the attacker, I'd know exactly who to avoid.

All afternoon my skin has crawled like we're being watched. That message I plucked from the dead woman's mouth plays over and over in my mind.

My shoulders ache with tension. The wedding is nearly over and there's been no attack, but it's coming. If the message wasn't warning enough, I can taste the threat in the air. Electric, thick, grimy. It crawls over my skin, an ever-present pressure, forcing me to stay alert.

"Anything?" Red says, sidling up to me. Because Octavia has spent much of her time with Queen Calandra and her council, Red has popped in and out, working with Daria and her team to offer support and hunter tactics.

I shake my head.

"Octavia said you had a wild idea about who it was."

I do. It's ridiculous given the levels of security. "I've got no proof," I say.

"Don't you? Octavia said you saw the marks on the girl's wrist."

I grit my teeth and drag her to the edge of the room, my eyes never leaving Penelope, who swings and twirls her sister around.

"The corpse had marks like someone had tried to bite her."

"Someone?" Red says.

My lips press together as if I can squeeze the idea away. "A vampire."

"In New Imperium?" she asks, checking over her shoulder to make sure we're not overheard.

"Yeah."

"That's not good. Shouldn't the fang marks have been obvious?"

"Not sure. It could be a failed transition. Or a vampire that was tortured and had their fangs recently removed. Your guess is as good as mine."

"Have you told Calandra or Daria?"

"Daria knows. All her guards are carrying stakes."

"Good move on the weapons. How the hell did another vampire get into the city? I thought the tunnels were mostly sealed off, and the ones we came through guarded or deserted. I didn't think anyone really knew of them," Red says, pulling a hand over her face.

"The real question is, if they are in the city, how do we stop them getting into the palace before Penelope is injured or Octavia's peace talks are ruined?"

Red leaves her expression stiff as she returns to Octavia. They clearly discuss what I said, because neither of them relax after that.

If it is a vampire at fault, then Octavia will be blamed, and that is the last thing she needs. It will destroy the progress we've made.

The longer the day wears on, the more agitated I become. Though both Red and Octavia continuously scan the doors, windows and any movement.

Dinner passes without a murmur. It's the most lavish meal I've ever seen served. Calandra even serves us goblets of blood herself. The most visible indication of peace to her nobles that I've seen yet.

I can't deny I'm famished. The hours and hours of heightened awareness, of constantly being alert is gruelling, even for a vampire. But this job is more than just body guarding. I want to protect Penelope. I need to. Something is coming and I have to be prepared.

I guzzle down the offering and then take a second helping of blood as the tables are emptied and the music ratchets up.

The beat kicks out, bodies move in synchrony as magicians, lords and even the occasional vampire prance around the dance floor.

Gabriel and Xavier have their hands up, wiggling and jumping about with a couple of Morrigan's friends; Jacob, I think one of them was called and Mal, was it? I forget, but they're chatting and drinking as they boogie together.

Everyone seems happy.

And yet my skin itches.

When I can't stand it any longer, I call out. "Red!" I have to shout it a couple of times over the crashing beats and trilling melodies. But I'm able to wave her over. She darts off the dance floor, leaving Remy and Bella smooching.

"Where's my sister?" I ask.

She points to the other side of the room where Octavia is talking with Quinn and Scarlett. It takes a couple of minutes, but I catch Octavia's eye. She mumbles something to Scarlett and heads over.

"Everything okay?" she says.

I shake my head and draw them both close. "I can't put my finger on it, but I want to walk the palace. It makes no sense. Everything pointed towards an attack today, right?"

Red and Octavia both nod.

"Will you keep an eye on Penelope? I won't be long, I just want to check a few of the weak spots, entrances and the like."

"Of course," Octavia says.

I break away, my eyes always darting back to Penelope.

She catches me leaving and a scowl falls over her expression. She grabs the nearest woman and begins gyrating her backside against the woman's groin.

A muscle ticks in my jaw. Doesn't she realise I'm literally doing my duty to protect her? I'm about to march over then and haul her off when a shadow rushes through my periphery.

I freeze.

My spine tingles.

It's them.

I know it.

I spin around, frantically searching the room. But there are so many magicians in here, the throne room is so ram packed with people that I can't tell where they went.

A sweeping movement. This time I just catch it. A hulking shadow. The same stature as the figure I saw in the nightclub.

It's definitely them. "Got you, motherfucker."

I lurch to the left, pushing and shoving my way through the throng of magicians to the edge of the room.

But I'm too slow.

By the time I reach the door, the shadow has vanished.

"Fuck," I bellow and punch the wall. My fist goes through the plaster. "Shit." I yank my hand out, hoping no one notices and head back to protect Penelope when I stop. There's a droplet on the ground. I kneel, swipe it up with my finger and sniff. Metallic. I lick it.

Definitely blood. Not just any blood, vampire blood.

Static rushes through my body, adrenaline flaring to life. I scan the floor, trying to dodge around everyone's feet. It's not just one droplet.

There's a path of them dotted every foot or so. Some of

them are smudged and smeared where feet carelessly tread on them.

"Shit."

In an instant, I'm up and running, desperate to find Octavia and signal the alarm. I push my pace right to the edge of vampire speed; I don't want to alarm the guests by displaying overt signs of vampirism, but there's no fucking time. I need to get to Penelope.

Octavia and Red stand just past the last magician in my path, and I jolt to a halt next to them. Thank the Mother of Blood they are still on alert, their eyes focused on Penelope and Morrigan.

"What is it?" Octavia says. Her expression is calm, but I can tell from the bite in her tone that she recognises my panic.

"Where is she?"

Octavia points to Penelope still dancing with her sister.

"Sound the alarm. He's here."

Red springs into action. "I'll find Daria." She vanishes nearly as fast as I arrived.

My skin prickles. The music speeds up, a thudding beat ringing through the room.

"Where is he?" Octavia says, her tone insistent.

I scan the room. Left. Right. Left. The door. The windows. Fuck. Where the hell did he go?

"Dahlia?"

I scan again. Faster. My eyes darting this way. That. FUCK. Where did he go?

"Dahlia?" Octavia barks.

I search faster. Finally. *Got you.* "There," I say, pointing at the shadow moving way too fast to be a magician. My body feels like lead as I track his movement and realise what he's doing: circling Penelope and Morrigan.

"Mother of Blood," I breathe.

"Go!" Octavia says, and we split up, moving through the crowds towards Penelope. I shouldn't have fucking left her. I never should have left her side, even to investigate. Gods dammit.

I ball my fists as I push and shove my way through the throngs of people. Always tracking the shadow. But as fast as I move through the crowd, he moves faster.

I'm not going to reach him.

And the deeper I push onto the dance floor, the further away Penelope seems to be. I want to shout and scream at her to get over here, but if I do, I'll alert the attacker. Or worse, set the crowds into a panic.

I'm almost there. Octavia too. She advances from the other side of Morrigan and Penelope.

But we're too late.

The music cuts out violently. A roar rents the air. The frivolity of the dance floor grinds to a halt.

There's one breathless moment of silence. A drawn breath held in the bellies of five hundred magicians. And then someone screams.

The shadow careens to a halt. His head is covered with a hood.

Time slows.

I bellow at Penelope to run. But she's frozen in place. She's not going to escape in time.

Something glints and I realise where the source of the blood I scented came from. A giant blade hangs from his hand, covered in the kind of coagulating rouge only discernible as one thing.

He lunges.

I leap.

The pair of us fly through the air towards her. The only thing that floats through my mind is regret.

Regret that I didn't tell her more. Didn't convince her we should try. Regret that I'll never get to know whether we could have made it.

He soars above the crowd and plunges down towards her, blade slashing out.

I know before the impact that I'm going to get hit, and it's not going to be good. But I don't care. I will not let Penelope come to harm.

I crash into Penelope, knocking her out of the way as I hit the floor. She screams. The shadow slams down on top of me, the blade swiping through my carotid. Blood sprays the crowd.

He leaps off me, turning to Penelope. I don't have time to deal with my neck: as long as my head is on, I'll heal. But the blood loss is making me woozy. I lunge up, grabbing at his ankles and tackling him to the ground.

We roll. Spin in a whirl of cloak, knife and blood.

Punches smash into ribs and guts. The impacts reverberate through the crowd.

His fists feel like iron. Each blow is excruciating.

Octavia rushes towards us, fighting through the now panicking and fleeing guests.

I haul myself up, though black spots speckle my vision. My skin is already healing, but I've lost a lot of blood. Too much. I slip on a puddle of claret as I scrabble to reach her and land on my arse.

I must black out for a second, because when I come to, he's standing over Penelope.

I don't think. My body springs forward. I scream as I fling myself through the air towards him.

Octavia is eight feet away. I'm going to get there first. A flash of silver winks in the dim light.

Penelope pushes herself up, a godsawful red mark on her cheek. That cunt hit her. Her eyes land on mine. She screams my name, horror written in the lines of her face.

But I realise too late.

My fist smashes into his temple, knocking the hood off as he spins.

The glint of sliver.

Too late, I realise I didn't block.

Too late, Penelope screams, "The blade!"

Too late, I recognise the man beneath the hood.

Silver plunges into my chest.

I rear back, falling, falling, falling. My eyes fall to Penelope. Even with horrors etched into her expression, she's still the most beautiful thing I've ever seen.

Everything quiets. A calm serenity washes through me as I gaze at Penelope. All my fingers and toes tingle, and I wonder if this is what desiccation is like.

I black out before I even hit the floor.

And then there's nothing.

CHAPTER 15

PENELOPE

I'm screaming Dahlia's name. But she's already turning grey as she hits the floor.

I storm forward, no thought to my safety or what I plan to do to the hulking man. I'm just desperate to reach her.

A boot slams into the middle of my chest. I'm flung back and crash into the floor. He pins me, pressing his filthy boot into my chest. The hooded intruder.

Only his hood has been knocked off.

Finally, I see his face and my blood runs cold.

His dark hair, lank and limp. Eyes beady and hollow. Skin paler than I've ever seen, almost as if...

He snarls, and that's when the truth slams into focus. Two incisors lengthened and blunted, as if someone shaved his fangs to useless stubs.

"Penelope," he growls.

"R-Roman? You're... you're a va—" I gasp.

He pushes his boot harder into my chest, cutting my words off and making me cry out. I can't breathe. There's a crack and a splinter of pain so acute I see stars.

Octavia careens into Roman, smashing him to the ground. I gasp for air, clawing at my chest, trying not to panic as I struggle to get oxygen in deep enough.

Red skids to my side, kneeling and grabbing my face in her hands. "Look at me," she barks. "Focus. Breathe slow. If you panic, you're going to hyperventilate and knock yourself out. Breathe with me. In. Out. In."

She's demanding, but it works. My heart rate steadies, and I adjust to the searing throb with every intake.

"D-Dahlia," I pant out.

Red pivots, spotting her lying motionless and dashes across the dance floor. She pulls the enormous blade from Dahlia's chest and shreds the fabric of her top to examine the wound. Red's expression is drawn, the lines of worry etching into her skin. And I can see why. Mottled veins plague Dahlia's chest. Oh my gods, is she desiccating?

Red bites into her wrist, shredding the skin and presses the dripping flesh to Dahlia's mouth. I struggle to my knees, about to go to her, but something heavy knocks into me. I'm sent flying and collapse on the floor several feet away. My ribs bloom again with an intense pulse of heat. Tears leak down my face. I'm screaming, but it sounds disjointed, far away.

Octavia and Roman are beating the shit out of each other. I've never seen a vampire move the way she does. Pure power. Blow after blow. You'd think she wouldn't stand a chance against a man his size, but she's hammering him. Pushing him back. One pace. Two.

I should be scared, but my attention is sucked away by something far more terrifying: Morrigan.

She appears, hovering over me, one hand open to help me up, the other brandishing two stakes.

"Are you ready to end this?" she says.

"Gods, yes."

"Then let's do it together. As sisters." She grins at me as the atmosphere around her shivers as if she's sucking power from the air itself. Her blue eyes burn like fire and flames. Threads of silvery magic peel from the palace walls, thick and fast. They swirl and swim around her, wrapping her arms and fists in power.

Fuck me, she's magnificent.

I yelp as she tears threads off her body and wraps them around me too. Power surges through my skin, melting into my fractured ribs and easing the constant, searing pain to a dull ache. My body is alive; energy and heat course through me. My gods, if this is half of what Morrigan experiences, no wonder she's obsessed with collecting magic.

We stalk towards Octavia and Roman. I risk a glance at Dahlia. Red is still feeding her as Quinn joins them, frantically unhooking a belt and pulling bottles and potions out.

But no matter what Quinn does, Dahlia's skin remains grey, those purple veins staining her chest. I have to bite the inside of my lip to prevent myself from screaming.

Scarlett sprints into the fray, katanas drawn as she joins Octavia. The pair of them move in tandem—Octavia with fists and fangs and Scarlett with swords crashing against Roman's weapons.

Scarlett takes a savage hit to the face and clatters to the floor. Octavia lashes back at Roman, her crimson eyes flaming.

The hits keep coming, reverberating around the throne room.

"Enough," Morrigan says and flings her hands out, contorting and twisting her fingers. Remy appears, her hands forming knots at a rapid rate. Bella too. The pair of them throw silvery strings of magic that bend and join each other, creating a lattice-like cage imprisoning Roman.

Scarlett, bleeding from her cheek, stands. She advances, wearing the same fury as Octavia. As she places her katana against his neck, she sneers the kind of rage that only a woman can wield. Octavia draws her fists back snarling, ready to pounce.

We work together as a team. Red and Quinn saving Dahlia. Remy, Bella and Morrigan holding Roman as Scarlett and Octavia guard him, ready to force him into submission.

Morrigan sweeps around to eyeball him. "We should have ended you when we had the chance," she says.

"And I should have killed you when you lay in my bed. Both of you," he spits, glancing between us.

"Who turned you?" Octavia's voice is so low, so filled with sharp edges it cuts the air like razors.

Roman laughs. "Get fucked."

"Force him," Scarlett says, holding her sword tight under his chin.

Octavia's tone changes; it melts into silk and rivers. "Tell me who turned you."

Roman's face relaxes into a compliant sort of daze. Is this compulsion? He shakes. But Remy and Bella's hands move faster, blurring into a haze. The lattice-like cage tightens around him, hissing as it sears into his flesh.

Roman screams out.

"Who turned you?" Octavia asks, her tone so deep, so rich, I have to fight myself from falling to my knees and answering for him.

Roman trembles as he fights not to answer. His nose drips steady rivulets of blood that cover his lips and chin.

Finally, he sags, his eyes dulling into a muted, distant expression.

"No one. Or they didn't change me knowingly. I swallowed some blood splatter in the club the night I had a visitor." His eyes slide to mine and I swallow hard. I'd managed to keep that quiet for so long. There are a few confused looks thrown my way, but thankfully Octavia drags everyone's attention back to Roman.

"Then how did you die? You were on a fixed regimen of transfusions to keep you alive," Octavia says. She uses the same silky, golden tone. It flows so smooth I think I'd do anything for her, tell her whatever she needs to know.

"Penelope visited one night and got close enough for me to steal a hairpin." He looks at me. I swallow hard knowing there will be repercussions from my little excursion.

Fuck. My fingers brush my hair, the memories drifting back. He made me lean close and then attacked me. He must have slipped a hairpin from me then.

"I used it to pick my cuffs. But I was caught. There was a fight. They drained me, but when I woke, I fought back, hard. Your bouncer, Erin, I think her name was, said she'd had enough of my shit and broke my neck. Silly woman didn't even know what she'd done."

A muscle in Octavia's jaw ticks. "And your fangs...?"

"I was disgusted with myself. You... your species disgusts me. Newborns aren't known for their self-control. I pissed off a gang of vampires." He shrugs, then winces as the lattice digs into his flesh.

But he continues, lost in the cadence of compliance. "They said my fangs would sharpen up eventually. But it left me hungry, pissed off and disgusted. It's Penelope's fault I'm like this, and there's no one's blood I'd rather drain than you two." He fires a filthy stare at Morrigan and me.

"Too bad," Morrigan says and hands me one of the stakes, nodding in Roman's direction. "You do the honours."

I take it and stare at the wooden spike. But I realise this wasn't just my fight.

It was both of ours.

He may have come for me tonight, but he came for Morrigan first. I take her hand and curl it around mine. "Let's do it together," I say.

We bring the stake up as Morrigan's silvery threads of magic weave around our conjoined fists. A surge of energy pools in my palm. I've never felt so strong. There's no coming back from this. Not for him. Not anymore.

Roman must realise this because he twists and contorts, fighting with every ounce of strength he has left. But Scarlett's katana cuts into his neck, and Remy and Bella's lattice prison tightens around his body, pinning him in place.

"Fuck you!" He shrieks.

Together, Morrigan and I plunge the stake into his chest. He screams, his skin flushing white and then he goes limp, grey and mottled veins spread over his skin as he desiccates before our eyes.

"It's over. It's finally over," I say.

Remy and Bella's hands cease moving. The lattice evaporates into the air, and Roman's body clatters to the floor. His skin is already flaking as I rush to Dahlia side.

"Is she..." I ask Red, but she won't look at me.

It's Quinn who answers. "It's not good."

CHAPTER 16
PENELOPE

Two days.

Two days of pacing, barely sleeping, barely eating. When I do sleep, it's in an armchair in the infirmary. I'm restless and fitful, my mind riddled with flashbacks, be they Roman, the Whisper Club, the body hanging in the doorway, the blade penetrating Dahlia's chest.

That's the one that repeats the most.

Over and over. And no matter how I try to distract myself, when I close my eyes, it's all I see.

Dahlia's siblings don't need to sleep the way I do, so they all sit in a state of stillness that unnerves me. They're conserving their energy so they don't need to feed. And given the bloodshed from the past couple of days, and the fact Roman had been turned, it's probably for the best.

By the third day, though, they reanimate, and this time, they're hungry.

Quinn, Remy, Bella and Scarlett all donate a pint of blood which Xavier, Gabriel and Red gratefully drink. Octavia refuses, she's still blaming herself and trying to ease out the political shitstorm that was unleashed after the wedding.

The one saving grace is that Calandra allowed Octavia and Xavier to compel every guest at the wedding to forget, save a handful of her council members. They are trying to get on. It's taking a lot of give and take and compromise, but their relationship has remained intact.

"How are you doing?" Red asks as I join her and Quinn outside Dahlia's room.

"I thought you said she'd be awake by now," I whine at Quinn. The exterior windows in her room are covered and darkened so no light filters through. But the inner windows through to the hall we're in are made of glass. Her siblings all rest in various chairs and positions like sentinels.

"I thought she would be too, but I'm not trained as a vampire doctor, I only have limited knowledge from the study I did." She squeezes my arm. "We did everything we could, but the fact she hasn't and isn't desiccating is a good sign."

Quinn and Red leave to find their friends, so I re-enter the room and sit on the bed holding Dahlia's hand. Time drifts, the room warming and cooling as the sun rises and then sets again. Someone brings me food, which I reluctantly pick at.

Sometime in the early evening, I take my place by Dahlia again and slip my hand into hers. I rub my thumb along the back of her hand the way she did to me at the ceremony.

She twitches.

I sit bolt upright.

"Dahlia?" I gasp.

Octavia rushes to my side, Gabriel too. He places his book on the bed and perches on the side opposite me.

"Is she awake?" Gabriel asks.

"I..." I say, but I don't know. "I swear her hand moved under my touch."

Xavier joins us now. "Come on, Dah, stop being dramatic and wake up."

Her hand twitches again. And finally, her eyelids flutter open. She squeezes her hand around mine, a slow grin pulling at her lips.

"Dahlia?" Gabriel says, leaning forward.

Dahlia's gaze flits to her brother. "Ugh. Penelope was a great view to wake up to. You... not so much."

He laughs and whacks her with the book.

"Oww, watch it, I was mortally injured, don't you know," Dahlia says, rubbing her arm.

"Yeah, she's going to be fine." Octavia smiles. "Glad to have you back, Dahlia. If you'll excuse me, I need to ready our carriage, we're all a little hungry to say the least. I'm sorry to pull you away so quickly, but I'm not sure how much longer I can last without feeding. I'm assuming now you're awake, your body is back to vampire speed and healing and thus well enough to travel?"

Dahlia stretches, cracking her neck this way and that. Her fingers paw at her chest, uncovering a silvery scar in the middle of her sternum. But she nods. "I'm good."

"Excellent, you have about ten minutes." With that, Octavia sweeps out of the room, and Dahlia's face falls as she locks eyes with me.

My stomach sinks hearing that they're going to leave so soon after she's woken. I thought maybe we'd get a day or two more while she recovered. But I forgot that vampires heal fast. Besides, we knew once the wedding was over there would be no need for them to stay.

Dahlia pushes herself upright.

Xavier ruffles her hair. She swats him and he beams at her. "Glad you're okay."

Xavier and Gabriel follow Octavia out, leaving Dahlia and me on our own.

"Hey," I say. My ears grow hot; my stomach is dancing in strange, agitated kicks.

"Hey yourself," she says.

But I don't know where we go from here. I don't know how to talk to her anymore. Everything is jagged and broken.

"Pen?" she says.

I can't bring myself to look at her, so I fiddle with the bed sheets. What if she regrets saving me? What if she doesn't want anything to do with me because it was my fault she was injured? I mean, she is leaving today, so what's the point in dragging any of this out? She probably just wants to be rid of me so that she can go back to her vampire city and find some vampire princess to be with instead.

"Penelope..." she says, more insistent.

"Hmm?" I focus on pulling a thread from the sheet. She tuts and sweeps me onto her lap and into her arms.

"Penelope Lee," she says, pulling my chin to face her.

"Yes," I breathe. Our lips are close. Where her fingers brush my jaw, my cheek, my throat, electricity brims under my skin. Like it calls to her. An insistent need that will go forever unanswered.

I want to close my eyes and fall into her.

"I..." Dahlia starts and then her words falter, falling away into the space between us. "I've had an amazing time," she says. But it doesn't feel real. It feels like a plaster used to cover up the truth of where we are. That we both knew this was fleeting. That once the wedding was over, it

—we, us, whatever we were for those few hours—would be over too.

And that's where we are.

My insides harden. I cannot and will not cry in front of her.

"I'm glad you're okay. I wouldn't have forgiven myself if something happened to you because of me," I say.

"How long was I out?"

"Three days."

Her fingers twine through the strap of my now filthy bridesmaid's dress. I really need a shower and change of clothes.

"You stayed the whole time," she whispers.

"Yeah..." And I don't know why she's asking these questions. Why she's dragging this out. So what, I stayed. It doesn't change anything. She's still a vampire. I'm still a magician. We're still from different cities, and it still won't work.

I shuffle off her lap as she gets out of bed.

Octavia reappears at the window and waves for Dahlia to join them before vanishing again.

"I have to go," she says.

I nod. "Well... thank you, for... you know. Everything. Guarding me. Taking a knife for me... For... everything else."

She makes for the door and then stops. My mind flashes back to that first night we met in the Whisper Club. It was me leaving then, now it's her. This way around is so much worse.

And just like I did, she returns, pulling me into her arms and plunging her lips onto mine.

She kisses me hard and soft, her hands skimming every inch of skin as if she's memorising me. As if she's touching every piece of me before she can't anymore. Her tongue

weaves its way into my mouth, caressing, stroking, ravishing. She moans into the kiss. And I hate her in this moment.
I hate her because as my legs weaken, she steals pieces of
me: my heart, my soul, my love. And in its place, she leaves
an indescribable agony. It cracks and splinters, sinking into
the fibres of my body.

This is the last kiss.

The last touch.

The last embrace.

I never wanted this. But I got it anyway.

I kiss her back, hard. Angry now. Pissed. My fingers claw
at her scalp, needing more of her, tugging her closer.
Wishing I could peel our bodies apart and stitch us together
as one.

We kiss for long enough my lips tingle and swell. I
refuse to let go. But it doesn't matter. Last time I pulled
away. This time it's her.

It's over too quick. I need more.

But she's by the door. She pauses, her back to me. Her
head tilts as if she wants to say something.

She doesn't.

The door clicks shut, and I am alone, one long, wet
streak running down my cheek.

CHAPTER 17
DAHLIA

TWO WEEKS LATER

I smack the body bag.

Jab.

Jab. Jab.

Left. Right. Hook.

Right upper cut. Left upper cut.

Sweat pools at the back of my neck and spills down my spine. I throw weights around the gym. Train harder. Push. Push. Push.

And at night, I drink. Drink. Drink. That has been my routine for two weeks. Just like normal.

Because everything *is* normal. Nothing has changed, save the small scar I now wear on my chest. I am fine.

Gabriel sidles into the gym in the basement of the Hunter Academy. I should stop calling it that, it's the unified army now but old habits die hard. He leans against one of the machines, book open, eyes darting over the page. But I can tell he's pretending to read. He follows me as I trail from weights to body bag to floor work.

"Spit it out, Gabriel," I say after this charade continues for another twenty minutes. I finish up a set of V-sits and stride over to him.

"It's been two weeks," he says, finally sliding the book into his suit pocket and stopping the façade. He looks incredibly smart today, a pressed red suit with an ornate black filigree design on the cuffs and collars.

"Right?" I say, waiting for him to get to the point.

"And on the face of it, you seem perfectly acceptable." He wafts a hand around, gesturing as he walks through the gym, lifting items with his thumb and index finger, his nose crinkling before he drops them again.

"I am fine," I say, leaning over a weight bench to do some dumbbell rows.

"And I'm sure Octavia, Xavier, and Red are buying that bullshit too. But I shared a womb with you, dear sister, and much as I prefer nonfiction, I've read enough romance novels to recognise a woman in mourning."

That makes me stop. "You've read romance novels?" I say, my face scrunching up.

"First, is it that surprising? I've spent five hundred years reading, you don't think I'd have at least dabbled in every genre they have to offer?"

I open my mouth and find myself bereft of any decent comeback. "Fair."

He drops an elastic band, his nose crinkled. "And second, I said 'on the face of it.'"

I narrow my eyes at him. But he continues his mono-logue, growing more smug by the second. Gods, I hate it when he's like this.

"You've been at work, gone to the gym. And in the evenings, you've been drinking."

"Exactly. Completely normal behaviour for me," I say,

knowing he hasn't got a leg to stand on and forming my own smug smile.

His eyes glint.

My smile falls.

"You haven't been fucking though, have you, Dahlia?"

Ah, shit.

"Not that I want to know anything about your love life. But usually, you're oh so liberal with sharing which girl you fucked on what night. And yet it seems you've gone two entire weeks and not a mention of anything. Now, unfortunately, it shames me to know this, but I dare say I've not seen more than three days in the last five centuries where you haven't had a tale of some whore or another to tell me."

I put the dumbbell down. He's got me.

He folds his arms. "So, are you going to explain? Or do I have to play the guessing game?"

I slump against the bench. Gabriel comes to join me, settling next to me and leaning on my shoulder.

"You are repulsive and smell like three-day old gym kit. But I can see that you need me. Praise me for being so gracious," he says and lowers his head to mine.

"Ever the dramatic, Gabe."

"Was it the princess?" he asks.

I sag against him, a heavy sigh billowing from my chest. "Yeah. It just sort of happened."

"That's the way it always is with love."

"Stop spouting your romance nonsense. It's not like I can do anything about it."

He lifts his head up and stares at me hard. "And why the hell not?"

"Come on, Gabriel. Be serious. She's a freaking magician princess. We've only just agreed to permanent peace, it's not like their city would accept us."

"And what about ours?"

I shake my head. "She's a royal. She can't just leave her city."

"I mean this with the greatest respect, but she's the spare. She has more freedom than Morrigan. You're making excuses not to try. What I don't understand is why."

He's right. I've run out of reasons. Fuck, I hate it when Gabriel is right.

"You know you need to go back for her, don't you," he says, nudging my shoulder.

"What if she doesn't want me? What if she won't leave her city? Or what if, in her mind, it really was just while we were there for the wedding?"

Gabriel gets up and makes his way to the door. He cocks his head over his shoulder and stares me right in the eyes. "I think the real question is, what if you never ask?"

CHAPTER 18
PENELOPE

Morrigan and Stirling are leaving for their official honeymoon today. They're going to be gone for a few weeks, and it's the first time I find myself a bit sad about my sister going off on her travels.

I stroll past her friends in the foyer and down the palace steps to their carriage. The sun is high, radiating warmth on my cheeks. It makes me wonder if Dahlia ever misses it, the sun, I mean. Which then reminds me of the afternoon we woke up and she nearly got burnt. Maybe she doesn't miss it. The way she would talk about the night and the moon made me think she loves it the way I love the sun.

Mother is clearly flustered about something, as she flaps around Morrigan and Stirling. She gives them both a kiss, hugging them tight before hustling straight back up the steps, waving at me as she passes.

"Gotta rush, Pen, I have a council meeting. We're opening the trade lines today. But I know how miserable you've been the last couple of weeks, maybe we should have dinner?"

"Sure, see you later, Mum," I say as I make my way to

their carriage. She's right, I have been miserable. Nothing feels quite the same since the wedding. The palace is calm. Roman is gone for good and yet, I don't know.

I'm just off. Out of sorts. Damn bored too, especially since Morrigan and I haven't even bickered once. It's probably just that. I loathe boredom.

Morrigan slides her case into the carriage and then turns to me. "Here," she says and hands me our nana's earrings. "It really did mean a lot to me."

"I know." I smile and slide them back in my pocket.

"I'll give you a moment," Stirling says, and gives me a quick squeeze before hauling her suitcase into the carriage, closing the door behind her.

Morrigan and I stare at each other not saying anything. It's awkward. My cheeks heat. We're not good at this, we only know how to quarrel. This is new territory, and I find myself fidgeting with my hands and toeing the cobbles.

"Oh my gods," she huffs. "Come here."

She grabs my shoulders and pulls me into a death grip of a hug. I laugh and then cough against her as she squeezes a bit too tight.

"I don't like seeing you sad." She strokes my hair.

"I don't know what you're talking about, I'm fine."

"Really? Funny, I'd say you were fine before the wedding, and now you're decidedly not fine. Almost like something is missing."

I shrug against her.

When she releases me, it's her turn to fidget. She dusts off her jacket and scratches her head before finally looking at me. "I wondered if maybe when we're back, me and you can spend some time together? Like, real time?"

I smile. "I'd like that. It's funny, but this morning I realised I might actually miss you while you're away..."

She grins and opens the carriage door, stepping up and pausing. "Only might?"

I indicate the smallest amount between my thumb and index finger, and she just rolls her eyes at me.

What used to be nasty jabs at each other now feels like loving banter. She heads inside only to poke her head around the door and say, "I don't know, Pen. I think you've found someone to entertain you just fine."

She blows a kiss and shuts the carriage door. I replay her words, my brows knitting together.

"Wait. What?" I say. But she doesn't open the door.

"Morrigan?" "What do you mean?" I bang on the carriage.

She pulls the curtain back and grins at me. Stirling's head pops up behind her. She winks at me.

I glare at her, my brow furrowing as deep as the tunnels under the city. "What the fuck does that mean?" I shout through the window.

But the pair of them just grin harder.

"Morrigan!" I shriek, but the carriage driver cracks the whip and the horses lurch forward, clopping against the driveway cobbles. I stare at the carriage while trotting after it. "MOTHERFUCKER," I yell.

The window drops, and Morrigan's hand sticks out to give me the birdie. I can hear her laughing even as the carriage disappears into the distance.

She knew? How did she know? I mean, sure I didn't leave Dahlia's side in the hospital, but it's not like we openly showed any kind of affection. No one saw her finger fuck me on the dance floor. The more I ponder her words, the more I realise what she was really saying.

"Almost like something is missing... I think you've found someone to entertain you."

She did know. She was telling me to go.

I stare at the path where the carriage was.

"Shit."

Night has long past fallen by the time I cross into Sangui City and make my way to the Whisper Club. I have no idea what I'm doing. How the hell am I going to find a single vampire in an entire city?

I figure I made it to the Whisper Club before and that's where we met, so someone there is bound to know how to find her.

But I don't even reach the club room. I put my hand on the club door handle and notice a strange little gargoyle creature staring down at me. I swear it moves, but I don't have time to check because the door swings open.

"What the fuck? I was just leaving to come to New Imperium," Dahlia says.

"Too bad. I got here first, and I figure you owe me," I say.

Her lips twitch, she raises an eyebrow at me, and I know it's taking every ounce of dominance she has not to grin. She hooks her finger inside the collar of my top and pulls me inside.

"And how do you work that out, Princess?"

I back up, she closes the gap.

The air around us ignites with electricity. Fuck, I've missed this. She hasn't even touched me and my skin is alive. My back hits the textured fabric wallpaper of the hallway wall. She places her arms either side of me, pinning me in place all over again. My stomach flutters. Her dark eyes are alight; those pools that sucked me in weeks ago.

That kept sucking me in during the wedding visit and pulled me back to her weeks later.

My lips part, I try to find the right words, but I'm all turned around. Jittery with the need to touch her.

"You told me that if you bit me while you fucked me, it would be the biggest orgasm of my life…"

"Mmm, I did say that." She licks her lips. I can feel the touch of her gaze dragging down my body, peeling my clothes off.

"You said we had to save it for another time. Well, Dahlia St Clair, it is another time. And I'm owed. So how about you fuck me, and bite me, and give me the best fucking orgasm of my life?"

She shakes her head and tuts at me. "Such a demanding little brat, aren't you?"

I suck in my bottom lip, fluttering my eyelashes at her. "How about I earn my orgasm? I believe you said it *tastes* like the best orgasm of your life. So how about I fuck you and you bite me?"

My fingers find their way to her trousers and unbuckle the button. She grabs my wrist and holds me there.

"I… I don't normally…" she starts.

I pull away, my cheeks flushing. I didn't realise she didn't want me to touch her. "Oh gods, I'm sorry. That's totally okay. We don't have to do that."

"No," she says. "I want to. Just. Not out here."

Lightning fast, she picks me up by the thighs, flings me over her shoulder and speeds us through the club. I squeal as she moves me faster than I've ever moved in my life. My hair licks out like coiled whips. We veer down a really dark corridor and halt outside a black door with a single blood-red droplet emblazoned on it.

Dahlia kicks the door open and barks, "OUT."

I can't see much around Dahlia's thighs, but I do feel the brush of several bodies as they abandon the room.

She takes us inside and then I'm dropped into an armchair. The room is blood red. Everything from the walls to the ceiling to the carpet and every chair, bench, and bed in here. The walls are lined with jars and toys and dildos and all manner of contraptions I've never seen before.

She stands before me, her jaw chiselled and her raven-coloured waves coiffed into place. She removes her jacket, followed by her shirt, then pulls her sports bra off over her head.

I reach out and tug her between my thighs, unbuckling and lowering the zip on her pants. I slide my hands in her trousers and under the band of her boxers.

"Are you sure?" I ask.

She nods and I pull them down until she tugs her shoes off and steps out of her clothes. I take her extended hand and she leads me to one of the beds. Her body moves like an animated marble sculpture, all lines and muscle and ridges. She's fucking exquisite.

We reach the bed, and I knock her onto her back and climb on top of her, plunging my lips over hers.

She kisses me hard before reaching down to pull my dress up and over my head. I didn't bother with underwear, not when I knew exactly what I was coming here for.

"Such a little slut," she says, rubbing her thumb over my hardening nipple. I knock her hand away. It's my turn and for once, she's going to do what I say. I slide down between her legs and then stop.

"You okay?" she asks, leaning up on her elbows.

"I, umm. Yes. I just. I forgot it's been a while, and I've only done this with one person before."

"Can you remember what I did?" she says.

I nod.

"Start there, and I'll guide you."

She slides her thighs open, and I bend to meet her pussy. I drag my tongue over her core, tasting every inch of her. I'm instantly wet. Gods, I forgot how delicious a woman is. I flick my tongue against her clit, slow at first. But lick by lick, I remember how to do it.

A little moan slips out as I lap up her excitement. She's tense, but the more I glide over her pussy, the more the stiffness eases out of her body. Until finally, she lets out a soft obscenity.

"Fuck, Penelope. Just like that. You love that, don't you?"

I hum approval against her cunt as I lap faster. I bring a finger to her entrance. "Can I?" I ask.

"Not yet, more tongue."

"Okay," I say and suck her swelling clit into my mouth. She bucks against me, wetness coats my chin as I lick and flick my tongue faster and faster. She grinds her hips into my face, and with every rocking motion, my own pussy clenches. Pulses of excitement bolt through me.

"I'm so close. Swing your pussy up here," she says.

I twist around and lay on her stomach, inching back until my pussy hits her mouth. "I'm going to bite you here." she strokes her tongue over the pulpy flesh where my thighs meet, "but not until I make you come."

"Okay," I say and nestle back between her legs, reorienting myself now I'm upside down. I tilt my head to get the right angle and resume swiping my tongue this way and that against her clit.

She lowers her mouth onto my pussy and I swear I black out. Having the taste of her on my tongue while she fucks me simultaneously is almost too much.

Pleasure washes over me, every inch of my skin pulses with molten electricity. She slides a finger inside me, and I gasp, not expecting her to be able to do it from that angle.

I can't cope, my pussy tightens, I move faster and faster, desperate to make her fall apart the way my soul is melting for her.

"Dahlia," I cry out.

She moans as I dig my nails into her thighs and drag my tongue as far down her cunt as I can reach.

She groans at my touch. My pussy tightens, I'm right on the edge. I swear she's holding me there on purpose.

"Finger," she says. "Use your finger."

I hook my arm around her leg and slide a single finger inside her. She's tight and wet and the feel of being inside her sends my body reeling.

"Oh gods, I'm going to…" I cry out as she slides her finger in and out of me faster, her tongue ravishing my clit.

"Ready?" she says.

"Yes, do it. Bite me."

There's a press of cold as her fangs brush against my thigh. A sting and then…

"Fuck."

My world explodes. She slides her finger in and out, to the same rhythm that she drinks me down. My eyes slam shut. My tongue flicks against her pussy once more. She bucks, groans and then her pussy clamps around my finger and she comes with me.

Colour drenches my vision. My body tightens, electricity shoots into every corner of my body. The orgasm hits my face, my mind. It fucking runs into my toes.

I am light. I am darkness.

I float in space, drifting on waves of gold and throbbing pleasure. The taste of her drenches my tongue. Every one of my senses is alive. I smell summer and winter and a thousand solstice nights. Ocean waves and blood moon skies.

It is endless.

I feel only pleasure for hours and weeks and years. Our bodies move together as she drinks and fucks and comes. Our orgasm stretches on and on until I am screaming and breathless and a boneless mess.

Finally, she releases me, licking at my thigh until it stings, and I assume, heals over.

She pulls me around until we're lying face to face.

"Well...?" she says.

"Yeah, you were right. It was absolutely the best orgasm of my life."

She smiles, smug, her dark eyes glimmering in the rouge light of the room.

"Told you."

I lean in and kiss her. The taste of me mixing with the flavour of her as I slide my tongue into her mouth.

We stay like that, caressing, kissing, her occasionally taking another drink, until the thing hovering between us swells and bloats into an ugly creature.

"We should talk," I say.

Dahlia strokes my shoulder in slow, gentle circles. "We should."

"When you walked away... I hated it. I've spent the last two weeks miserable."

"Me too," she says. "And I really was on the way to find you. But I don't have any more answers than I did at the end of the wedding. How do we make this work? You're a princess. I'm..."

She gestures at herself.

I wipe a smear of my blood off her lip. "I think that if we both want this, then we can find a way to make it work.

Even if that means long distance temporarily until we can figure out how I can move here."

She nods. "I'd like that."

"Besides. You're mine now."

That makes her eyes flash. "Oh, no. You are sorely mistaken, Princess. The only one owning anything in this relationship is me."

She spins me onto my front and straddles my thighs, her hands hovering above my ass.

"Dahlia!" I shriek.

"Penelope," she growls out my name as a warning. "Say you're mine..."

"You just said this is a relationship. I might not be the greatest magician, but that math says you're mine too." I grin.

She brings her hand down on my arse.

Smack.

"My brat," she snarls.

"My vampire," I yell back.

She smacks my other cheek and then she releases me, sighing.

"Your vampire," she says and holds out her hand to let me up. I beam at her as she finally admits defeat.

She *is* mine.

Today. Tonight. And fuck, I hope forever. I take her hand and brush my lips against hers, teasing. Tempting. Taking. I know I'll be punished for this later. But it is *so* worth it. I can't help the grin as I smile into her kiss and whisper against her lips...

"Your princess."

STIRLING

THE NIGHT OF THE WEDDING

We've been married for hours, but not yet a full day. I've been waiting for a moment alone with my wife for what feels like a vampiric lifetime. We were pulled from pillar to post all day. Meeting guests, speeches, the dancing. And then after the attack, it was all security debriefings and councillors in uproar until everyone who wasn't rational had been compelled to forget.

It's finally past midnight, the throne room has been cleared up, the guests sent home and Daria has calmed her tits about security.

At last, it's just me and my... wife. Gods, it feels good to say that.

We draw to a stop outside the throne room.

I sling an arm around Morrigan's waist and grin at her. "The last time I found you here at this time of night, I remember a rather indecent evening."

"Mmm," she says, her words silky smooth. "I seem to remember you worshipping your queen, as you rightly should have."

"Ahh, yes. I think I negotiated a rather wonderful reward from what I can remember."

Her smile is playful and sexy as she pushes me against the throne room door, pinning me in place. She runs her hand through my hair, pausing at the back of my head and pulls me to her mouth.

Her lips cover mine, smothering me in kisses. Deep, wanton and needy, her tongue slides over mine.

She tastes like love and light. Like all the stars in the universe and a little like forever.

"Gods, I am so in love with you," I whisper as she pulls her mouth off mine.

Her hand reaches behind me and unlocks the door. The throne room is so much quieter now it's empty. Shrunk back to its normal size, too.

Sat on the dais are three lonely chairs. Three thrones.

"There's three?" I ask as Morrigan shuts and locks the door behind us.

"Of course," Morrigan says and slips her fingers through mine, guiding me towards the new throne.

"Whose is it?" But I already know the answer. She leads me across the room and up the dais staircase that only a few hours ago, we walked up single and down married.

Once we're on the platform, Morrigan raises our joined hands and kisses mine. "You're a royal now, Lady Grey..."

"Well. I... I guess?" Albeit only through marriage. But I suppose it counts? We were banished for so long, stripped of our magic for so many years that I'd rather stopped thinking of myself as a lady and instead saw us as one of the people.

I stare at the throne; this new one is different to the other two. Morrigan's and Calandra's are golden and jewelled in rubies, gems, crystals and ornate, intricate swirling filigree.

This chair is... "My gods," I whisper as I really take it in. It's made of the same golden stone as the other two. But instead of gems and crystals, a blue colour sweeps the back, licking up and curling into waves brushed with a white marble-like stone. It's as if the throne is made of a wave lifted from the ocean. Carved into the back of the chair is a rather familiar sailing boat.

"Oh..." I say as I peer closer. The boat isn't just a boat; it's my boat. My eyes sting instantly. It's stunning. Blue sapphires kiss the hull of the boat and disappear into darker-coloured navy gems.

I'm silent for so long that Morrigan slides her hand into mine. Her voice cracks, a tremble lining her words. "Is it... is it okay?" she asks.

"It's the most beautiful thing I've ever seen." I fall to my knees, just like I did last time. Ever ready to worship my queen on my new throne.

But Morrigan shakes her head. "Not this time. Tonight is all about you."

"Oh," I say again, incapable of much else. Seems I've been incapable of many words today, my eyes too obsessed with the sight of my new wife.

"Strip, Stirling," Morrigan says, suddenly serious.

I tilt my head at her bossy tone, thoroughly enjoying the fact she's taking charge. I raise an eyebrow, wondering what she'll do if I disobey.

"Don't test me," she says as if in answer.

My lips purse into a cheeky grin as I unbuckle my

trousers. I turn around showing her my back. "You're going to have to help me out."

She grabs the silky ribbons keeping my corset tight and tugs them, her fingers press and pull and yank until the corset is loose enough I can tug it over my head.

I'm topless, because who needs a bra in a corset? Morrigan's fingers trail down my back making goosebumps rise over my flesh.

"Undo me," she demands. Gods, I love it when she embraces her authority. I do exactly as she requests.

My hands glide over her corseted waist as I pull the silk ribbons keeping her in locked inside her dress. "Who tied you in here?" I whine. It's fucking impossible to get her out.

Morrigan pulls a knife out of her waistband, "I figured you'd struggle," she says and hands me the blade.

"You were just carrying that?"

"Well, after this evening, do you really blame me?"

I guess not. "Does it matter if I shred it?"

"Not if it means getting me out of this fucking thing, it weighs a tonne." She wriggles in the dress, which is more like a sculpture than an outfit.

I tuck the blade between her back and the ribbons and slice. Morrigan lets out a relieved huff as the corseted top of her dress pings wide open. She wriggles and stretches, revealing the mottled impressions of corset bones pressed into her tattooed skin.

She steps out of the dress and hurls it out of the way, leaving her in black lace underwear. I swallow hard. My mouth waters almost as much as my pussy.

Morrigan's fingers caress my skin, her tips padding over my chest and flicking over my nipples.

"Do you remember what happened last time we were here?" she says.

I inhale in anticipation as I recall that night. "You were sat on the throne, I was at your feet, and I worshipped my queen."

She nods. "Underwear. Now."

I dutifully obey, slipping my undies off and glancing back at the throne room door as if staring from this distance will confirm it's locked.

Morrigan swings me around and shoves me. The backs of my knees hit my new throne, and I drop into the seat.

"Magnificent," she says and then my glorious queen kneels beneath me.

"Morrigan," I gasp.

But she's too busy mauling her way up my calves, nipping and kissing in equal amounts. Her fingers dig into my thighs as she wraps them around my hamstrings and tugs me to the edge of the chair.

"Spread," she demands.

Her voice is commanding. It makes my body melt, my mind compliant. She raises herself onto her knees, pushing between my legs and leans up to kiss me. I reach around and drag my nails down her back. Her nipples and those silver bars react, tightening into peaks. As her tongue pushes into my mouth, my thumb brushes over her breasts.

She moans into my mouth and slips her hand from my legs to my core, drawing two fingers down my centre.

I whimper. "My queen."

"My wife," she replies.

Her fingers circle my clit, over and over, until my thighs burn, my own nipples tighten, and I am gasping against her kiss.

"So wet for me," she says and places a single kiss

against my lips. Her fingers push inside me. My head rolls back as I cry out her name.

"Fuck, Morrigan." It's all I can say as she drives inside me over and over. Her free hand pushes me until I rest against the back of the chair. She nestles between my legs, her tongue finding my clit and drawing over my throbbing apex.

"Oh gods," I pant. My hips buck against her mouth as I grind against her. I open my eyes and stare at the sight of my wife between my legs. Her eyes lock onto mine while her tongue laps at my pussy, her breasts rocking with the movement of her fingers inside me.

It's enough to make me come undone. But Morrigan slows, she's clearly not done, intending to prolong my pleasure.

She licks hard and then soft, drawing her hot, wet mouth over my cunt until I'm bucking and screaming out, desperate for her to make me come.

As my walls clench against her fingers, she stops thrusting. My eyes widen, I was right there.

"What the...?" I say, ready to whine.

But she reaches beneath the throne and pulls out something that was taped to the underside of the seat. It's long and thick.

"Oh," I say. "Oh, I see."

She slots her legs into the straps, pulls the dildo into place and tugs me off the throne. She's careful to hold on to me as my legs shake from the pressure of an almost-orgasm. She swaps places to sit on the chair and tugs me over her lap, positioning me right over the head of the dildo.

"I think you need to break in your throne." She grins,

grabs my thighs and presses me down onto her lap, spearing me with the cock.

I moan as it thrusts up into me. Morrigan grips my hips and forces me to ride her.

"Fuck," I whimper as I slide my arse up and down, up and down. She supports me with one hand and then slips her other hand between us to rub my clit.

"I may have always been your queen, but now you are mine."

"Oh gods," I rock my hips against her lap, grinding harder and harder as her fingers move quicker. Her lips find my nipples, licking and sucking until my body shivers with pleasure.

"My queen," she breathes against my breasts. She flicks her fingers against my pussy, driving me closer, my body vibrating higher and higher. I'm panting, a line of sweat trickles down my spine as my thighs burn against the rhythm of riding her.

"Come for me, Stirling," she says and sucks my nipple into her mouth, grazing her teeth over my peaked flesh.

At her words, I spill over the edge, my eyes roll shut and my body breaks apart. I cry out her name as my pussy clenches around the dildo. I rock once, twice, three times more before collapsing on her.

We stay twined together, kissing and adoring each other until the dawn birds sing outside the palace windows.

I make Morrigan fall apart with my tongue, and she pins me to the dais floor, riding my face the same way I rode her lap. She fucks me against the stairs, then on the floor. I worship her on her own throne, repeating the actions of that night all those months ago.

Over and over, we make each other come. Each time

whispering secrets and confessions, adorations and soft words of worship.

It is everything a wedding night should be and so much more. Finally, when the first sounds of the palace waking up drift in from the corridors, we haphazardly dress and make our way to her rooms. There isn't much time: our carriage leaves early this morning. We have two weeks of meet-and-greets and royal events around the city before we can honeymoon. Calandra has us on a relentless schedule before letting us 'swan off' as she put it.

The team waits for us in the palace foyer, Scarlett beaming with pride as she looks at me. "Can't believe my younger sister made it down the aisle before I did."

"Yeh, neither can I," Quinn says, shoving her out the way and pulling me into a hug. "I hope you have the most amazing honeymoon."

"Where is it you're going again?" Remy asks as Bella appears behind her.

"We've got two weeks of duties to do first. We'll head back here for a goodbye dinner and then we'll start out in Nefari City, before heading to the fae isles."

"Nefari?" Bella's eyebrows nearly climb off her forehead.

"You know it?" I ask.

"Yeh, sort of. Why would you go there? I heard it's full of the worst kind of people," she says.

I nod. "But the worst kind of people make the best kind of magic. I've got a very old, very powerful grimoire to negotiate for. It's my wedding present."

"You can't call it a wedding present if you haven't actually got it," Quinn says, her face scrunched.

"Have you ever known me to lose a negotiation?" I fold my arms and stare at her.

She opens her mouth but doesn't find anything to say.

"I thought not."

Remy puts her fist out for me to bump. "Be good, kids," she says in the most un-Remy like slang. Maybe Bella banged some of the stuffy professor out of her.

"When you're back, I want to tell you all about this new runic—"

"Let me stop you there, Rem, why don't you tell Bella, hmm?"

Remy eye rolls at me. "One of these days you're going to need my skills."

"For now, I just need your friendship."

She smiles at me and pulls me in for a proper hug. Morrigan and I give each of the girls a hug in turn and then head out to the carriage.

Queen Calandra gives us both hurried goodbyes and then Penelope joins so I give her and Morrigan a minute. But even as we're settled in our seats, Morrigan curled under my arm, I can still hear Penelope shrieking at us as the carriage rides off.

"You think she'll go?" I ask.

"Did you see the way she looked at Dahlia? Of course she will," Morrigan sighs and rests her head against my chest.

"The real question is, can you get the grimoire? Bella is right, you know. That city isn't a great place. It's run by the mafia."

"Did you forget who you married?"

"I'm just saying."

"And I'm just saying I can negotiate for anything. I won your heart, didn't I?"

She jabs me in the ribs.

"No more relationship deals, remember? You made your last one with me."

"I did." I nod in confirmation. "Besides, I have something much better now..."

"Oh?" She sits up to look at me.

I grin my most charming smile, the one reserved just for Morrigan.

"A promise."

She frowns.

"A promise to love. And be loved. Today, tomorrow, next week, next year. To love you until I'm nothing but ashes and sand."

And when I say the last line, she says it with me. "Until our souls find each other again where blue meets blue."

Not Ready to Say Goodbye to Dahlia and Penelope?

If you loved A Game of Vows and Vendettas and need more of Dahlia putting this bratty princess in her place, you're in luck.

A Game of Brats and Brides is a bonus smutilogue that takes you beyond their happily ever after. Watch as this vampire bodyguard and her princess navigate what happens when "mine" becomes official.

Expect:

- Dahlia's dom energy at its finest
- Penelope's bratty mouth getting her into delicious trouble
- All the spice you could want
- And just what happens when a certain question gets asked...

Get your signed copy on:
https://www.rubyroe.co.uk/products/bratsandbrides

ABOUT THE AUTHOR

Ruby Roe is the author of lesbian fantasy romance. She loves a bit of magic with her smut, but she'll read anything as long as the characters get down and dirty. When Ruby isn't writing romance, she can usually be found beasting herself at the gym, snuggling with her two pussy...cats, or spanking all her money on her next travel adventure. She lives in England with her wife, son, and two devious cats.